"Listen," Hogan stood before him, hands on hips, scowling a little. "If what I think is true you have more than the patrol to fear now, boy. . . . "

"But what have I got to do with your quarrel with the companies on Fenris?"

"Fenris! Fenris is the first, but perhaps the least of our objectives. We're snarled up in half a dozen webs, all being spun by some busy spiders working for opposite ends and with the stickiest means they can manufacture out of their devious minds. If we come through the next week or so and take away even one one-hundredth of the stakes on the table, there'll be action to rock more than one system. Freedom for Fenris . . . great nebulae! We're fighting for freedom for a whole species—our own!"

SECRET OF THE LOST RACE

ANDRE NORTON

SECRET OF THE LOST RACE

ACE SCIENCE FICTION BOOKS
NEW YORK

SECRET OF THE LOST RACE

An Ace Science Fiction Book / published by arrangement with
the author

PRINTING HISTORY
Eleventh printing / May 1985

ISBN: 0-441-75836-3

Ace Science Fiction Books are published by
The Berkley Publishing Group,
200 Madison Avenue, New York, New York 10016.
PRINTED IN THE UNITED STATES OF AMERICA

Confidential: X3457-A-R-
From: Kronfeld, Director, Colonization Project 308
To: Lennox, Commander, Space Scouts, Fifth Sector,
Detached Rating.
Subject: Service Files.
Require release to this department service files for follow-
ing:
   O-S-S-D 451 Marson, H. Deceased.
   O-S-S-D 489 Ksanga, V.T. Deceased.

Confidential: X3457-A-R- Reply
From: Lennox, Commander, Space Scouts, Fifth Sector,
Detached Rating.
To: Kronfeld, Director, Colonization Project 308
Subject: Service Files
  Regret orders forbid release of official records to any
department not connected directly with service.

(Message in code from Lennox to Sen Yen Lui, Commander-in-Chief, Fifth Sector, accompanying micros of
above)
  What is going on? Who talked and where? Should these
files be "lost" for the duration?

(Reply in code: Sen Yen Lui to Lennox)
  Sit tight. We will ask questions of our own. If there is
trouble shall contact you at once so you may take proper
steps.

Order: 56431-S.S.D.

From: Mahabi Kabali, Space Admiral, Commanding Fifth Sector

To: Sen Yen Lui, Commander-in-Chief, Space Scouts, Fifth Sector

Subject: Service Files

You will herewith order release of records of following (listed below) to be consulted, in accordance with usual procedure, by Kronfeld, Director of Colonization Project 308.

O-S-S-D 451 Marson H. Deceased
O-S-S-D 489 Ksanga, V.T. Deceased

(Coded note accompanying the above)

Sorry. Pressure is on, hard. We can not sit on this now. Anyway both men are safely dead, and have been for years. And there can not be any possible leak of the real facts; only suspicions.

(Call on private com band from Kronfeld to Bryar Morle, Port of N'Yok)

Get your best private investigator on this. We know now that the probable port of entry *was* N'Yok. And there was a child that looked young but was about six or seven. Time of entry approximately fifteen—sixteen years ago. Sure, the trail is cold, and it's getting colder all the time. But this is our first positive lead; it could well be the last. I needn't tell you that this is a category one order. Time is running out. Draw on the Foundation Funds. We can prove our case if we have the evidence. Those boneheads in uniform are already sweating!

(Comment of Bran Hudd, partner in Hudd and Rusto, Private Investigators.)

Cold trail? This thing's in space freeze now. What does this joker think we are—miracle men or time travelers? Rusto: He lays down the credits like he grows 'em special in his cellar. So we go through the motion anyway. And a spread of cash can loosen tongues. You have that mock-up of what they think the dame looked like. Shove off and start earning our share.

JETTOWN, PORT OF N'YOK, where strange wares were sold for the amusement, fair or foul, of crewmen out of space, and those who preyed upon them, and the elite who took their cut from the predators in turn. There were circles within circles on the streets, an intricate social organization which would have amazed the city dwellers beyond the rigidly drawn, yet physically unmarked, boundaries of that sinister blot edging out in a triangle, its base fronting on the scarred landing aprons, a narrow tongue licking "uptown."

On the streets a man's life might depend not only on his wits and toughness of body, but also on the development of a sixth sense of impending trouble. Sometimes an uneasy foreboding swept the whole area. That eerie disturbance was alive tonight, though the hour was early and few of the big spots were fully open.

Kern's SunSpot was, but the boast of the SunSpot was that it never closed. The air, tossed about but not in any manner really renewed by the conditioners, was tainted with old smoke, the aroma of weird drinks, and the old, old smell of over-crowded humanity. The big central room was as always with Step and Haggy on duty at the bar. A few of the girls were already drifting in.

Yet the young man, seated alone at the star-and-comet table, his counters in a neat rack before him, the unopened packs of kas-cards at his elbow, checked the highly illegal force-blade in the soft folds of the wide silken sash about his flat middle. His shoulders moved under the loose-sleeved jacket which covered his ruffled shirt as if he were flexing his muscles in prelude to some attack. Trouble—he could taste it, smell it—this was going to be a bad night.

He snapped on the play light above the table. Under that carefully adjusted radiance his thin face was that of a boy, wearing the faint, indecisive cast of adolescence, almost of youthful innocence. That face was worth a lot to his employer. Kern valued Joktar for his face, as well as for the keen brain behind it, and the clever, knowing hands which obeyed that brain. Kern trusted his head star-and-comet dealer as far as he trusted anyone—though that was a limited distance.

Joktar knew that his game was checked at intervals, and that a variety of sly traps had been set for him. A good many dealers in the SunSpot had come to sudden and sometimes messy ends. At least three had been delivered to the Emigration men. Kern had seen to it that all his employees were made fully aware of such object lessons. So far Joktar had run straight, not for any ethical reason since ethics were not learned on the streets, but because playing a straight game with a vip was simply good insurance.

He admired Kern's executive abilities without developing any personal liking for the man. And so far the boss of the SunSpot was the only stable thing Joktar had known in this dangerous world. He had been at the SunSpot most of the life he could remember, which was a short one for he did not even know how old he was. Though strangers always undercalculated his age by a half a dozen years or more.

Since that peculiarity added to his value to Kern, he welcomed it. Though when some buck lost at the tables and turned nasty he was apt to try to take on the "kid" for an easy smash. Accordingly Joktar had acquired a well known and respected proficiency with a force blade, and had other knowledge of odd forms of personal combat learned from tutors who had picked them up all around the galaxy. As a result Joktar of the SunSpot was now reckoned one of the deadliest infighters on the streets, though he was no call-out man with a ready challenge.

Click, click, the counters with their emblazoned stars, their glittering diamond-paint comets, moved under his slender fingers. He built a small tower, lowered it chip by chip. Every nerve of his was responding to the unseen menace—waiting.

"The E-men are out. . . ."

That was a whisper from beyond the table light. Joktar glanced up from his pile of counters. Hudd, the banker from the one-two table, stood there. He was a new man, but too much of a pusher. Joktar gave him another week here, perhaps a day or two more, then he'd push too far, ask one question too many and Kern'd take steps. He wasn't a police plant. So he must be a spotter from one of the other vips; somebody could be planning to pull a climb-up on Kern. Joktar smiled inwardly. How many had tried that game in the past? Almost as many as the counters in his racks. Kern had had a long run and no crack showed yet in his organization.

"They're sweeping?" he asked Hudd as if it did not matter in the least.

"The growl is that they're going to make a big pull."

A big pull. And the news passed to him by Hudd. Joktar added one point to the other. Could this be an oblique warning? Why? Hudd was no friend of his. So why did this newcomer wish to pull any of Kern's men out of an E-net . . . unless he had a future use for him. Only . . . Joktar had not been approached lately with any offer to change allegiance. He always reported such to Kern, knowing that at least half were tests. This a new one?

"Pass the word." He stubbed the light button, swept his card packs and counters into the wide drawer of his table and sealed them there with the pressure of his thumb in the lock slot. He stood up, slim, small, boyish, his cool eyes surveying Hudd with aloof speculation.

The other met that stare with a calculating intentness, as if the younger man was a hand held by a too-lucky player. His lips parted as if he would add to his warning. But Joktar had already turned away with the controlled litheness of a blade man, to cross to the lift which served Kern's private apartment above.

Orrin was on guard aloft. A stocky, solid man, not yet run to seed, trained as a space marine before he left that service under circumstances which made him useful to Kern. Orrin whirled, his blaster half out of the holster, as Joktar stepped from the anti-grav plate. He laughed a little raggedly, and slapped his weapon back.

"Better sing out on the way up next time, kid. A man can lose half his brain pulling a quiet come-in like that."

"You got the jumps? Well, the signs are up . . . trouble."

Orrin's boots shuffled, his broad face was unusually sober. "Yeah, there's a few! You got a nudge for the boss?"

"Maybe so, maybe no. Call me in."

Orrin snapped the lever of the visa-plate, waved Joktar before it. The whirr of the answering buzzer came as a panel slid into the wall. The dealer flipped the force blade from his sash into Orrin's waiting hand. For anyone to pass Kern's door armed was to face inanimate sentries who eliminated without question. Human guards could make mistakes, Kern's last line of defense never did.

"What's the rumble?"

Kern's lank form sprawled on an eazee-rest. His voice was soft and the tone came from his thin, concave chest. He was dressed in street-finery. His lavishly embroidered brightly colored clothes did

5

not hide the angular lines of his ungainly body. Similarly, his long, curly, gray-brown hair, and the thatch of sideburns that grew to exaggerated points on his sunken cheeks did nothing to soften his sharp features. He pointed and Joktar sat down on a footstool—a concession.

"Nothing as yet," the dealer answered the question.

Kern's silence was an invitation to elaborate.

"I have it that the E-men are on a big pull."

"Yes," Kern yawned. "That would stir up the streets. Who spilled? One of our runners?"

"Hudd."

"Hudd. Well, well, well. Did he make this growl to you personally?"

Joktar smiled, an engaging, boyish expression, until one noted the coolness of his eyes. "He was meant to, wasn't he?"

He fully expected agreement from Kern. Every time he had spotted one of the boss's checks, Kern admitted readily enough that the test had been his idea. But this time the other shook his head.

"Not my hand, boy."

"Hudd's a plant," Joktar stated firmly.

"Certainly. But for whom, and why? Such small mysteries make life interesting. We'll let him run on the string a little longer until we discover who holds the other end. So he made a point of warning you. . . ."

"I haven't had any offers recently." Something in Kern's expression brought that out of Joktar, almost against his will, and he felt self-contempt for offering that avowal.

6

"I know that. How long have you been here? Fourteen . . . no, it must be fifteen years now. And yet you still look like a dewy-eyed kid. I'd like to learn that trick, it's a neat one for our business. Yes, it was back in '08 that that doll staggered in here with you pulling her along. You were a smart brat even then. I'd like to know where you came from."

An old crawling chill touched Joktar. "You had me psyched, didn't you?"

"Sure. And by a medic who knew his stuff. All he got from you was babble about a big ship and the port here. That doll was queer, too. I sure wish she hadn't died before Doc could run her through the hoops and really learn something. Doc swore you'd been blocked, that you'd never be able to remember more than he got out of you under a talky shot."

"Why did you keep me here, Kern?"

"Well, boy, I like puzzles and you're about the best I've ever got my hands on. You grow a little bigger, but slow, and you keep looking like a kid, yet you've got a brain that ticks fast and straight and you don't get smart ideas. You're about the best dealer I've ever seen spread out the cards. You don't take to dames, nor to rot-gut, nor to happy-smoke. Just you stay the way you are, boy, and we'll rub along without any flarebacks. So, this growl is that the E-men are out? Set up the house warning."

Joktar went to the panel of switches on the far wall, pulled three. Throughout the SunSpot now the general alert would go up. Not that Kern should have anything to fear from an E-raid, he paid in enough each quarter to equip fifty colonists and that was a matter of official record.

7

"Could it be Norwold, I wonder? He's been reaching lately. If he's due to get the blast. . . ." Kern squirmed out of the soft eazee-rest. "Tip that flutter to Passey, he's our spot-man at Norwold's tonight. Tell him to be ready to flit if there's a raid, but also, he's to watch where Norwold plants those two new dolls—we could use 'em here."

"Right." Joktar went out, collecting his blade from Orrin as he passed. He wondered about Kern's guess that Norwold would be netted. You *could* buy your way out of the E-pens, but the price was so high only a vip or a vip's favorite could unpocket enough. The E-men raided to obtain the cheap labor needed to open up a frontier planet. Colonists volunteered, passed rigid tests; emigrants were dispatched by force: neither ever returned. To be caught in an E-raid was the most blighting fear which overhung the streets: processed, drugged, sent out in frozen sleep from which some never awakened, to endure slavery on an alien world.

Colonists were heroes. To be an emigrant one merely had to be alive, reasonably healthy, and in possession of an undamaged body—undamaged that was in the sense that one had the proper number of arms and legs. A good many men on happy-smoke went out in deep freeze. Supposing he was netted, would Kern unpocket to get him out of the pens? He doubted it.

Joktar was on the anti-grav plate when the alarms went, setting up a noiseless vibration which tingled through the flesh, nerves and blood of every man and woman under that roof. *Raid, E-raid–here!* So, Hudd had given him a straight growl after all!

8

He slammed his hand against the controls of the grav plate, sending it up instead of down. Too late to try to reach the low runs. There was only the roof way.

But he slowed the plate at the third level. What about Kern? Orrin waved him back when he would have gone to the boss's door.

"Boss says scramble!"

The guard crowded on beside the dealer. Kern, alone, of those in the SunSpot had the power to negotiate with the raiders. But how had his espionage system failed so badly that they had been jumped without any real warning? Was Hudd in E-service? No, he wouldn't have given a warning if that were true. Joktar asked a question of Orrin. He shrugged. "Don't ask *me* where the snap came, kid. For all I know the boss pulled this flareback himself. He didn't spout any fire when we got the alarm."

Joktar's brain chewed that. He could see no possible cause for Kern to open the SunSpot to raiders. On the other hand the boss had a love for the devious which could be satisfied by this roundabout way of removing some subordinates. Joktar thought of the more prominent employees, trying to pick out any Kern might hold in disfavor.

The plate came to a stop and Joktar's palm flattened on the wall where the heat of his flesh, as well as the patterns on his finger tips, unlocked a door for them. Ahead was a narrow corridor. The tingle of the alarm snuffed out. Orrin snorted.

"They must be close. Let's hope most of the boys made it in time."

At the end of the corridor a series of toe and finger

holds led them to a climbshaft. Topping that they would be directly under the roof. Of course the E-copters would be waiting up there, but the refugees would have fog bombs to handle that situation.

"You got a good lay-up, kid?"

Joktar's sixth sense pricked. Why did Orrin ask that? Every employee of Kern had his own hiding place for the raids.

"Any reason not to try the regular?"

"Dunno," Orrin sounded uneasy. "Just wondered . . . if the boss did set this one off . . . well . . ."

Yes, Kern could have betrayed every bolt hole, every hideout. The trouble was, as Kern's man, he had no choice now. He'd have to follow the set pattern of escape already learned. All other avenues would be the property of Norwold's crowd, or Dander's or Rusanki's and so closed to outsiders.

"Better speed up, they'll be puffing soon," Orrin warned.

Yes, the raiders would loose narcotic gas into the building, following that with the "shake-up" of sonic vibration: an efficient combination to clean out the building. Joktar pulled up to the section where he crawled on hands and knees under the shell of the roof. It was dark here, he would have to locate the fog bombs by touch.

His outstretched hand swept across a row of egg-shaped objects. Joktar wiggled one free and nursed it in his left hand, his other going to the blade in his sash.

He hunched close to the end of the passage, his shoulders now under the trap door. Heaving it up an inch or so he looked out. The glare of raid lights dazzled his eyes. Bringing the small bomb up to that gap he triggered its control and rolled it out.

A second egg followed the first. Then there was a pain twisting at him nerve and muscle: a warning of what would be agony in seconds to come. The sonics were on below.

"Get going!" Orrin shoved him. The fog was curling up from the eggs, cutting down visibility.

"Now!" Orrin's hand at his back half propelled him through the trapdoor. Apparently the ex-marine was more sensitive to the vibrator.

Joktar was in the half-crouch of the experienced knife fighter. The fog formed an envelope about them, a mist into which E-men would not dare to blast for fear of shooting their own men.

The dealer made for the far side of the roof. He must swing over, out, and down; a way not to be taken blindly by anyone who had not practiced that maneuver. Then, a short dash to another concealed door and the rest of the escape route tailored to Kern's orders.

Joktar leaped into the whirling blank of the cottony mist. He lighted on solid footing, sped on to the door. There was no sound of Orrin behind, perhaps the guard had not dared to make that jump into nothingness. For a moment the dealer hesitated, and then the first law of his jungle prevailed: in a raid it was each man for himself.

A panel swung under his hand. He plunged through only to be pinned in a spearhead of brilliant light. Joktar's last coherent thoughts, as he went down under the full impact of a stun ray, was that he

must have been included on Kern's list of expenda-
bles after all.

Joktar did not open his eyes at once. He let the
senses of hearing and smell relay the first information of his new quarters to his brain. He knew he was
not alone; a moan, a grunt, a querulous mumble to
his left, assured him of company in misfortune. The
smell of closely packed and none-too-clean humanity backed up that deduction.

He concentrated on his last clear memory, he had
burst through the proper bolt hole, straight into the
arms of a reception committee. So, now he must be
in the E-pens. For a moment wild panic shook Joktar's control. Then he forced himself to open his eyes
slowly, to lie still, when every inch of him, mind and
body, clamored for action. But his first lesson on the
streets had been the need for patience—that and the
folly of fighting against overwhelming odds blindly
and without plan.

Letting his head roll to one side he obtained a floor
level view of his present quarters. Haggy from the
SunSpot lay next to him, a drooling thread of saliva
spinning from his slack mouth. Haggy, and beyond
him was a stranger wearing the grimy skin which
spelled happy-smoke addiction.

There were two more, both strangers and drifters.
the sort easily swept up in any E-raid. But to find
Haggy a fellow captive, that meant that more than
one bolt hole of the SunSpot had been tagged. Haggy
was not one to linger after the alert was on. Were all
of Kern's senior employees here?

Time was one factor which must be reckoned

with. Joktar tried to remember whether there had been E-ships waiting in port. But then such a raid usually occurred only when there was a ship ready. No use housing and feeding emigrants at government expense.

A man might escape from a planet-side prison. However as far as Joktar had ever heard there was no escape except a buy-out from the E-pens. Unless you could prove that you were an honest citizen in good standing with a job. They were careful on that point nowadays, ever since the big stink when they had swept up the son of a councilor who had been doing some sight-seeing on the streets and shipped him off to the stars. Now there was supposed to be a double check on the status of emigrants and that was when a buy-out could be arranged. But for that a man had to have someone working from the outside.

Kern? Joktar considered the possibility of help from the boss. He thought there was a thin chance, a very thin one, of that. And a man clung to any chance at a time such as this. He had no weapon, they had taken his knife, and the very possession of such a blade would count against him. His hands explored—yes, they'd taken his purse, his other small belongings. But what he wore beneath his shirt, the one thing which he had carried out of his misty childhood, that was still on him.

"Attention!" That impersonal bark out of the air overhead was like a whip-snap. "You will come out through the door immediately!"

2

As a section of the wall opened Joktar felt the warning twinge of a vibrator. The captives would leave, all right, or twist in agony. He got to his feet, stooped to shake Haggy. The barman moaned, opened bleared eyes which became terror-stricken as he grew aware of his surroundings. Lurching free of Joktar's hold, he staggered to the door. The dealer followed, to be caught up in the web of a tangle field. He could still walk, in fact he had to, since he was being drawn down a brightly lighted corridor, but otherwise he could not raise a finger.

The E-men had all the props. But then, why shouldn't they? The Galactic Council was solidly behind this emigration policy which worked two ways. First it got rid of the drifters and those outside the law on the civilized worlds, and second, it helped to open new planets. Thus both problems were

SECRET OF THE LOST RACE

settled to the satisfaction of all but the victims, who had no political power anyway.

Haggy had passed through another door ahead, now it was Joktar's turn The barman was in the process of stripping off his gaudy clothing under the supervision of a bored medic.

"All right, you there," the same man spoke to Joktar, "strip."

Joktar regarded him mutinously. They had relaxed the tangle field, but if he tried to jump the medic, they would slap it on again and they could tighten those lines of invisible energy to choke the breath out of a man's lungs. No use fighting when there wasn't the smallest chance to win. He dropped his jacket, unwound his belt sash. No chance to palm anything since they must have a spy spot on him. But, as his shirt followed his jacket, the dealer's hand went to the disc hanging on a chain about his throat.

"Hand that over, you!" the medic was alert.

For the first time since the momentary panic upon his awakening in the pens, Joktar's control came close to snapping. He stood breathing a little raggedly. The medic clasped one hand into a fist and Joktar staggered, bit his lip against an answering cry. That vicious squeeze of the tangle was a warning. He tossed the disc to the medic, who allowed it to fall to the floor and kicked it away spinning.

So he was processed after Haggy, run through the examination machines, his brain busy with escape plans as impossible as they were fleeting. Then, wearing a coverall of coarse red stuff, vividly visible, he was steered into a cell with five others, all strangers.

16

They were fed from mess kits slid through a wall panel. And there was little talk among them. These were all young, Joktar noted, but of the drifter class, spineless hangers-on such as could be picked up by the hundred in the streets. He squatted back on a bench, the mess tin on his knee.

"Hey!" one of his cellmates sidled down the bench. "You worked for Kern, didn't you?" There was a malicious twist to his half-grin. The gap between his sort and a man who was employed in one of the big spots was an ocean wide.

"Me, I usta run for Lafty 'fore he got wiped off the books," he added in a spurt of half-defiance. "Saw you in the SunSpot layin' 'em out. Think Kern'll unpocket for you now?" His grin grew wider.

Joktar shrugged, chewing methodically at the tasteless mess on his plate.

"Kern got wiped proper," one of the others raised his head to sputter through a full mouth. "Saw four—five of his men being run through here."

That could be true. Though how such a coup could have been managed with runners and spotters planted to prevent just such a catastrophe Joktar did not understand. This report dimmed his one small hope of rescue. Kern himself might be in the pens now. Who was behind it, Norwold?

"Anybody heard where they're fixing to send us?" The thin voice shook a little.

"Ship in port bound for Avar," volunteered the ex-runner.

"Yeah? What's Avar, anybody know?" another of the captives asked.

"Field work," someone answered, but he didn't

sound too convincing and Joktar was sure that was a guess. Perhaps because field work could be preferred over labor in a mine.

The ex-runner gave a laugh which was close to a snarl. "Don't matter much, burnout—you goes where you is sent. No pickin' or choosin'. You ain't no colonist. When you lands here your luck is out anyway."

That was only too true. Someone sighed and Joktar finished the last of his food.

"They freezes you, don't they?" the quavering voice asked.

"Sure thing," the ex-runner responded with a ghoulish relish. "No room in an E-ship to have you sittin' round eatin' your fat head off. Stick some needles full of goop in a fella, make him stiff as a board, and bed him down in a hold. He'll keep 'til you get planet-side again."

"Only I heard as some don't make it to wake up again."

The ex-runner leaned forward on the bench. "Sure, a man's luck may be run out all the way. They gets enough of 'em through to make a trip pay. Maybe them machines they had us in and out of tell 'em which can make the big jump and live."

"Hey!" One of the others started away from the wall. "I hear someone comin'! Maybe they'll run us out now."

Joktar was on his feet, his mess tin held as if that could serve him in place of his lost force blade. The ex-runner laughed.

"Fixin' for a rumble, kid? You ain't got a chance. Every guard in here carries a tangle. Me, I'd take what they dish out peaceable. No use askin' to be worked over just to prove how big and brave you are.''

He was right, but Joktar resented that rightness. His own helplessness was a frightening thing. He had believed he was tough and independent. But he began to realize now that there had always been Kern and the SunSpot between him and the full rawness of the streets. Now he was really alone and he needed time to adjust. He put the tin plate on the bench, seated himself beside it. And the ex-runner, reading his face with the shrewdness of his kind, stopped grinning.

A guard stood in an open panel, surveying them with open contempt. His glance fastened on Joktar and he beckoned. The hope which had died a few moments earlier revived. Kern, buying him out? Joktar shoved past the ex-runner, only too willing to obey that summons. The familiar strangle of the tangle fell about him and his spark of hope flickered.

Two more guards closed in at the end of the corridor and one of them spoke to the man escorting the captive.

"Gentlehomo Ericksen wants you at the front office. We're to hold this one until later."

"Why the change?"

"Space port police want to ask him some questions."

Space port police? Joktar was bewildered. Was this some move of Kern's? The boss had his contacts in the port control, all vips did. But, as the first guard left, the tangle caught with a painful grip about his middle.

"Get going, you!"

The pace they set was close to a run and Joktar sweated, his first uneasiness growing close to fear. These guards had a furtive air, as if they were acting beyond their orders. Yet their attitude toward him did not suggest they were in Kern's pay.

His puzzlement grew as he was hustled into a small room to front a man in the uniform of the port police as well as a young man wearing a tunic Joktar had not seen before. The regular space patrol went in dark blue, this man's garb was silver-gray and sported a badge bearing a glittering constellation, instead of the comet and circle of stars. Joktar blinked. Somewhere—perhaps in that portion of his brain which had been blocked so long ago—a small prick of warning flashed, then spread. He knew that this stranger spelled a deadly danger out of all proportion to their present meeting.

Then he glimpsed what the strange officer was holding and sucked in his breath. The disc he had been forced to abandon in the examination room swung from its chain gripped between the other's forefinger and thumb. Above it the man's face was stark with anger. Yet Joktar was sure he had never seen the other before.

"Well, gentlehomo," the policeman spoke first, "this one of the scum who jumped you and your friend?"

"If he isn't, he knows them! This proves it, doesn't it? How else would a burnout from the streets get a scout's ident? You—" he added two descriptive expressions which flattened Joktar's lips against his teeth in a tight snarl. Then the dealer rocked under a blow across his face.

"Well? Speak up! Where did you get this ident?" In its way the policeman's reasonable tone was as deadly as the open brutality of the officer's attack.

"I've always had it." Joktar was startled into the direct truth and knew that they would never believe him.

One of the guards who had brought him there spoke hurriedly:

"Look here, we'll have to make this quick. They've ordered him up to the front office. There's a buy-out waiting."

The officer in the gray tunic stiffened. "Who'd unpocket for this dirt?" he demanded. "Talk you, and straight on orbit! Who burned down Kender last week? And where did you get his ident, you swine?" He swung the disc as a flail and the metal ripped Joktar's already bruised cheek.

When he shook his head, as much to combat dizziness as to deny the charge, they really went to work. He was helpless in the tangle and they battered him until at last he lay on the floor, trying to hold to the ragged edge of consciousness, still bewildered. There was a bustle at the door.

". . . ordered to get him to the front office. He's been cleared."

Cutting across that came a hot protest from the officer. "He's not going to get away so easy. He's one of the gang who mugged Kender, and he's going to pay for it."

Again the reasonable policeman: "If we hold him legally, we'll have to have more proof than just that ident disc. He could have bought that from some stumble-bum for the price of a drink. And how do you know he didn't?"

"Wouldn't he have said so? This story about its being his—these things don't just float around in free fall, you know. One is given to a man when he swears in, and he doesn't lose it easy. Kender was dead when they ripped his off. Why this little scum could trade on that ident anywhere, saying he was on detached duty, and live high!"

"But you'll still have a time proving murder on him."

"I tell you he isn't just going to walk out of here!"

There was an amused chuckle from the policeman. "No, you've seen to that. The boys'll have to carry him."

"Yeah," the guard sounded morose. "We take him upstairs looking this way and there'll be a beef blowing us higher than the first Moon base."

"Look here," a new voice said. "How about this, we're loading 'em in the *Griffin* right this minute. Slip him in with the rest of that bunch and who'll care afterwards? Just a mistake on somebody's part. They can't reach out and grab him out of space, and the front office won't speak up if there's likely to be a stink. He can't do anyone any harm where the *Griffin's* going."

"And where's that?" demanded the space officer.

"Fenris."

The name meant nothing to Joktar but he detected an appeased note in the other's answer.

"Fenris!" The officer laughed. "That should do for him all right. Can you get him out on that ship?"

"If we hurry him through. And what if he doesn't get all the shots? Who's going to care if he doesn't wake up on the other side?"

The last thing Joktar heard was the judicial reply the policeman:

"Seems like you boys have it all figured out. No, I guess no one is going to worry. This whole thing's off record, remember. And you'll have to cook up a tale to satisfy your front office. Me, I'm not going to be dragged into any hassle with them."

They gathered their victim up from the floor and that pushed him over the border of unconsciousness. When he half aroused again he had been dumped on a flat surface with force enough to set his body aching.

". . . stupid fools. Bring in this one late . . ." voices ebbed and flowed over him.

"What happened? He looks to me like an accident case."

"You aren't paid to ask questions. Probably a fight in one of the pens and this one started it. They hauled him out to keep the peace. We get enough of those."

Hands were stripping off his coverall. There was a sharp stab of pain, then another. A persistent buzzing, then black and cold—a cold so intense he shriveled, as a man shriveled under a force blade slash.

Joktar did not know or feel when he was rolled from the table into that waiting box with an unhealthy resemblance to a coffin, when the lid of that was made fast in impatient haste with skimped attention to various dials and indicators. A placard was slapped on the top, and the box became one of many in a truck waiting to roll.

Then came the space port where the transport

waited under the crane projecting from the E-ship's hatch. The jaws of the crane bit into one box after another and they swung up, over into the maw of the cargo hold, each to be pegged down in a niche from which the cargo would eventually be discharged alive or dead as chance willed it. This would be months later in planet time and half the galaxy away in space. The last box was wedged in, the hatch sealed.

Not too long afterwards, the ship trembled to the push of jets, arose on her tail flames, moved out on course.

In the E-station front office a man waited with a packet of credit notes. He grew impatient, demanded action, at last made a closed-com call to a number which surprised, irritated, and faintly alarmed the man in whose office he waited.

Another man, also equipped with credits, heard a rumor in the waiting room, confirmed it in two surreptitious and hurried interviews, and left the E-station. He debated the necessity of the return of the credits to their proper owner. And, because he was not foolhardy, he went back to the streets, found a hideout and admitted to the man there that certain plans had gone wrong. The man named Kern was disappointed enough to take several steps in the direction of retrieving his own prestige by a few sharp lessons. But once those orders were given he forgot the whole affair for awhile.

A third man in a small, discreet office, received a com call. As a result five men in widely separated points on Terra found themselves embarking on new assignments and three took off by jet for N'Yok.

Two E-guards were questioned, shipped out for Melwambe Port after being warned that if they talked they were going to be given the same processing they had given others. This was done within the month in spite of their protestations. The service could not stand another scandal, not now when there was an alarming new stirring behind scenes. Both E-guards eventually reached a planet named Blore and within the year one died from pal-pest and the other was killed by his fellows for informing on a gang break.

Another man, in the gray uniform of the scouts, went to a jeweler's shop in N'Yok the same hour the *Griffin* lifted. He had an ident disc forced open. But when he read the name inside he went white under his space brown, remembering certain old stories. He was tempted to drop the disc into the nearest rubbish disposal when he left, but he finally decided to see it destroyed in his ship's atom-break. On his way back to the port his pocket was picked. When he discovered his loss he was frightened, thoroughly frightened, for the first time in years.

A councilor, making a wide-flung inspection of frontier planet conditions, was scheduled to visit the second planet of the star, Zeta Lupi, in the Wolf Constellation. The name of that world was Loki and its closest neighbor was Fenris. There were hints of trouble on Fenris.

In an outlaw camp on Fenris a man challenged the mob boss for a blast out. The man was named Samms and had once been an emigrant, now an escapee from the alibite mines. At present he nursed a long range plan and the call for a blast out was the second move in it. Because the day was an unusually cold one and his opponent had been running a trap line, Samms was a fraction of a second faster and became the leader of the Kortoski mob that night. (Report from Hudd and Rusto, N'Yok to B. Morle, redirected to Kronfeld, Director, Colonization Project 308)

Subject was questioned by space scout, disc taken from him, later opened by jeweler. Ident was for Marson, O-S-S-D 451. Scout took disc away from him. Thought subject was responsible for fatal mugging of his partner, Kender, which occurred on streets three weeks ago. Must stress difficulty dealing with E-station. Believe records there purposefully suppressed. Kern also tried to buy out subject.

(Closed com between Kronfeld and Morle):

Kronfeld: Put men on this space scout. I don't altogether buy this friend-being-mugged story. Might just be something else. The boys in gray are getting upset all along the line. I want a full report on this scout. Will deal with the E people myself. Forget Kern, he's out of the picture now.

(Interdepartmental com)
E-S 59641—7/20
From: E-Service Station, N'Yok Port, Irson, Agent in charge.
To: Kronfeld, Director, Colonization Project 308.
Subject:

Report concerning emigrant, male, age about eighteen, race, Terran, picked up in raid on SunSpot, fourth day of March.

This man shipped out on E-ship *Griffin*, destination planet Fenris for service in alibite mines. Correctly attested "unlawfully employed, unnecessary to the well being of Terra." Micro of record attached.

(Closed com, Kronfeld to Morle)

K: Are you sure this is the man? Record from E people way off on age alone.

M: They omitted some facts turned up in his physical, too. This record was edited. Certainly wrong on age, I have witnesses who can prove that. But if you are right there would be such a difference. They're working hard to cover up the irregularity in his ship-out. But he was the one sent to Fenris all right. What can you do about that?

K: Nothing until he arrives. I'll alert our agent there. Trouble is that is a critical point just at present. He would land in a place such as that! With luck we may be able to bid him in at the auction. Fenris! It !ooks as if someone would like to get rid of him just as badly as we want to pull him into the fold. Blast those damn scouts. This was badly muddled straight from the beginning. I hope Thom and Cullan can roast their tails straight up their spines! Send me everything you can dig up as fast as the boys feed it to you.

(Excerpt from Galactic Guide)

Fenris: Third planet in the system of star Zeta Lupi, Constellation Wolf. With the two other planets in this system, Hel and Loki, it shares a climate and terrain hardly endurable for native Terran stock.

Principle export: alibite and some furs. Traces of earlier native race, now extinct, exist in form of stone work and mounds. Subject to severe storms and nine months of freezing winter weather per solar year. One port: Siwaki. Two towns: Siwaki, Sandi, center of mining territory. Posted by survey as unsuitable for tourist travel. An "A" certificate required from anyone engaging passage to Siwaki.

At another camp, on the other side of a small mountain range, a spaceman who had been cashiered from the service and only recently had been bought out of a labor gang, listened carefully to the man who had put up the credits for his release. Then he talked himself, describing an event in his own past in detail. His benefactor was thus enabled to fit another piece into a very wide and broken puzzle, rounding out a pattern to please the man in the discreet office on Terra.

But the *Griffin* rode on, snapped into hyper-space, carrying in her cargo the missing element which would influence movements from Terra, to Fenris, to Loki. And an ex-star-and-comet dealer from the streets began the first step towards realizing a bizarre future.

3

ABOUT THE PORT of Siwaki the landscape was almost lunar in starkness. Only the harshness of the jagged peaks which enclosed the cup of the valley were muffled—one could not say softened—by a thick growth of vegetation on the lower slopes. This vegetation existed in the cold months as odd sponge-like skeletons with stem surfaces which could withstand even a tri-steel blade, and was a slate-blue in color.

That blue stain spread up to meet the snow. And always the cold bit deep, through thermo underclothing and furs, through the heated walls of the living domes, stinging inward to a man's bones.

Fenris was alibite. Men went to the mines, ore came back. A fringe of businesses based on that two-way traffic made up Siwaki. And there were a few fools mad enough to try trapping for furs in the river valleys. But they were only a handful, the remnants of men who had pioneered Fenris before the companies fastened their strangleholds on the port and the three-quarters-frozen world.

This morning four of those independents had paused to scan the notice of an E-ship auction posted on the government board. Two of them shrugged, one spat eloquently, but the fourth continued to read on into the fine print of the clipped code of governmental language, until one of his companions tugged at the sleeve of his outer fur coat.

"No use trying to buck that."

The reader's eyes, which were all that showed between the shielding roll of lamby wool about his hood and the frost mask covering nose and mouth, still held to the poster. Although the outdoor garb of Fenris added bulk to the body it covered, there was a hint of youthfulness in the way he shook off his fellow's hold.

"We'll stay," he spoke flatly, the authority of his tone not muffled by his mask. The man with him shrugged, but his mittened hand rested on the second belt about his middle, the one which supported the universal blaster of the frontiersman and a twenty inch knife in a fur tufted sheath.

At that moment the numbed cargo mentioned in the poster was beginning to revive. Joktar, his memories of the E-station very hazy now, heard the muted chorus of mutters, moans, and such other symptoms of distress as he had heard in the N'Yok pens.

"This one's breathing."

He was grabbed, armpits and feet, swung out on a flat surface. Swift jabs of pain, then he was flung back to the misery of full revival. For misery it was, as the torture of returning circulation carried with it a belated realization of where he must be and why.

Sitting up, he blinked at the lights in the room, rubbing his hands over his bare body as if their pressure could relieve the tingling. For some reason he seemed to have recovered more quickly than the rest, for of the twenty men lying along the shelf-like projection, he was the first to move freely. Memory supplied a name . . . Fenris. Just a name . . . he had no idea what kind of world lay outside the walls of this room.

"Stir up!" Men appeared in the doorway, wearing coveralls with the symbol of the port service on back and breast. They worked with rough efficiency to rouse the rest of the captives. Joktar sat where he was, a dull hatred seething inside him, wise enough not to resist. But his desire for escape was fast crystallizing into a drive almost as basic as his will to live.

The head guard reached him, gave a half grin as he surveyed Joktar's slim body.

"The E's must be baby snatching now," he commented. "You'll end up on the bargain counter, sonny."

"All right, all right! On your feet, you dead heads!" The captives were pushed into a ragged line. "Get these on."

A duffel bag was produced and from it the guards pulled small bundles of cloth, tossing one to each man in line. Joktar drew on the pair of shorts, snapped the belt cord about his narrow waist.

"Mess . . ." They were pushed past the door,

31

each handed a pleasantly warm container. Joktar felt real hunger, twisting off the top to swallow down a thick liquid, half stew, half soup.

"Now get this!" The head guard mounted a platform at the end of the room. "You're on Fenris. And this is no planet where you can go over the hill and live to get away." He snapped a terse word to his underlings and they put up a video projector. "There's only two places a man can live here. Right at this port, and up at the mines. You try to blast off, and this is what'll happen."

At a second snap of his fingers a series of vivid video scenes appeared on the wall above his head. If the horrors they pictured had been faked, the creator had had a very morbid imagination. Joktar did not believe that they had been. Every stark detail of what could happen to a runaway was there in three dimensional color: blanket storms, lamby on the prowl, poison springs, and half a dozen other terrors native to this wolf world. Even breathing without any protection meant that the icy crystals in the winds could bring a quick and fatal lung disorder. As a lesson against escape the show was very forceful. But the pictures did not in the least modify Joktar's private plans to stage a breakout at the first opportunity.

"Now you're going up for auction," the guard told them. "You'll probably be mine fodder. Play along with the rules, don't try any tough stuff, and you can maybe buy your time some day. First ten of you, this way."

By chance, Joktar was numbered among that ten. He was hustled on into a larger room, standing with his group on the platform facing a small audience of perhaps a dozen or so. Most of them were seated at ease, their outer furs slung back. But there were three or four others to the rear of the room who did not look so much at home.

". . . certified fit and able for labor . . ." someone droned. A man in E-service uniform was reading from the ship record.

The Fenrian guards thrust their charges into line again. One by one they took a man by the shoulders, turned him slowly about for the inspection of the buyers. As they reached him, Joktar heard a voice rise from the bidders.

"What's that kid doing here? Nobody could get a full week's worth out of a skinny little worm like that!"

"I dunno, Lars, those skinny ones sometimes are tougher than you think." Another man arose and came forward to the edge of the platform. "Let's see your paws, kid."

The guard didn't give the Terran time to obey on his own. Clamping a grip on the captive's elbows, he swung his arms out. The bidder stabbed critically at the nearest palm.

"Soft. Well, that'll harden up using a digger. Might make a sorter of him. Only they'd better take a mark down on his price."

Joktar was shoved back into line and his neighbor brought out. The bidding began and, when they reached Joktar once again, he saw one of the men by the doorway move forward.

"Ten skins, prime lamby," the words broke through the monotonous offers of credits. The man who had examined Joktar's hands swung around in his seat, scowling.

"Who let this woods beast in?" he demanded.

The newcomer continued to thread a way between the seats until he stood by the E-officer.

"E-auction, right?" he asked, his tone holding much the same bite as had that of the mine man.

"Yes." The officer was plainly bored by it all.

"No privileged bidders, at least the notice didn't say so."

"No privileged bidders."

"Then I offer ten prime lamby skins." He stood there, his feet in their fur-lined, fur cuffed boots, slightly apart, his body balanced as if he were about to issue a call out for a blaster meeting.

"Ten prime lamby skins bid," repeated the E-officer.

"Fifty credits!" snapped the challenging company man.

"Fifteen skins."

"One hundred credits!" a second of the miners cut in.

The E-officer waited a moment and then spoke to the other. "You still interested?"

Joktar watched the newcomer glance to his fellows by the door as if in appeal. When there came no answer from them, he shrugged, walked back. A snicker arose from the company men.

"Stay out in your mountain dens and freeze!" called the victorious bidder. Then he turned to the business at hand. "Well, do I get him for a hundred?"

The E-officer nodded and Joktar became the property of one of the companies.

They were sorted out into company groups at the end of the sale, fed, given quarters for the night, and each a suit of thermo clothing. Joktar listened eagerly to the guards, treasuring every scrap of information. He was now owned by the Jard-Nellis Corporation and their holdings were in a newly opened sector edging into the Kamador mountains; he had not been particularly fortunate. He tried to learn something about that other bidder, but discovered only that he was a trapper and that his bid was probably only another move in the old struggle between the companies and the handful of men who had pioneered Fenris on their own.

Early the next morning the emigrants were loaded into the cargo hold of a crawler bound for the mines. Aircraft was not practical on the wolf world. Freakish storms had brought about too many crashes during the early days of settlement. Now transportation followed the archaic modes of travel, the roads themselves patrolled constantly against washout and storm damage. And against something or someone else, Joktar surmised, when he assessed the number and quality of the weapons carried by an unnecessarily large number of guards riding the crawler.

None of the emigrants were the type to rebel in order to break out into the highly inhospitable wilderness they had already been indoctrinated to fear. So why the guards? And blasters and needlers were no protection against storms.

The heavy vehicle ground away from the port, but the emigrants in its windowless middle section had no view of the countryside. Fifteen men, drifters from the streets, happy-smokers already sunk in the gloom of a cut-off addict, a couple of bruisers who might have been the personal guards of some vip, shared those cramped quarters. The bruisers Joktar studied until he decided that they were not the stuff from which rebels were made. They might instead, if they survived the initial months of breaking in, serve as guards over their fellows.

As the men in the crawler began to shake down into a gang, he held aloof. Already the muscle men were asserting themselves. Joktar did not fear having to face either of them alone in rough and tumble, he knew too many tricks of infighting. But the two of them together would be a different matter.

The long day ended when the crawler sheltered for the night at a way station and the men were hustled from its warm interior, through a chill which bit like acid, into a dome. It was then that Joktar learned something new about himself. That cold which ate at his fellows, even subdued the bruisers, did not strike at him with the same intensity. His thermo suit was no better than theirs, and he had none of the outer furs of the guards. But to him that change of air was more exhilarating than numbing.

He thought about that as he swallowed the canned stew, remembering one or two other odd happenings out of the past. Those summer days in N'Yok when Kern had rallied him on always appearing cool; he had not been able to understand why others of the SunSpot staff swore at the heat every time they were forced to venture out of the aircondtioned building. And another time, further back when the cook, crazy mad from drinking sar-juice, had locked him, then only a small boy, into the freeze room. The dark cavern of the freeze room had scared him some but not the cold. When Mei-Mei, Kern's current favorite, had found him, she'd been scared too, but because he had walked out under his own power. At the time he hadn't understood clearly what had excited her so much, now he began to. Suppose he could stand extremes of both hot and cold better than most men?

If that were true, it became a point on which to build an escape plan. He was so intent upon his thoughts that he momentarily forgot his surroundings. Then a foot struck against the knee of one of his out-stretched legs.

"You there, bones, pay attention when a man talks."

Joktar glanced up. This would have come sooner or later, he had been resigned to such trouble ever since he had sighted the muscle men in their group. They were making the old, familiar play of the streets. Since he was, to outward appearances, fair game, someone they could belt around as an object lesson, they were going to put on a show. But neither was armed and it looked as if he had only to take one at a time.

A hand pawed at him, fastening thick fingers in the front of his thermo suit. Joktar yielded to that pull with a willingness the other had not expected. What followed was a complete reversal of the attacker's intentions.

The ex-dealer caressed skinned knuckles with the fingers of his other hand, and stepped over one flattened body to meet the snarling rush of his late assailant's partner. But a voice from the door of their lockup startled them both.

"All right you jet-propelled muckers! That does it!"

Joktar didn't need the jerk of a tangle to halt him.

He stood quietly, enveloped by the invisible cords, while the guard crossed to him.

"You," the company man stabbed a finger at Joktar, "over there." His order was enforced by a pull from the tangle. "Since you have so much energy, we'll just make you a load-hop on the jumper." His words meant nothing to his victim, save that the Terran did not doubt they meant a change from the crawler, and so perhaps a thin chance for eventual escape.

"The rest of you," the guard used another tangle as a lash, sending them reeling backward, "walk small, or you'll be cut down to size the hard way."

He motioned Joktar ahead, out into an open space where a much smaller copy of the crawler stood.

"Take a good look," he bade his prisoner. "That's a jumper, used to supply the prospectors' holes back in the mountains . . ." He waved to the peaks murkily visible through the dome. "You try to travel outside her belly and—" a click of his gloved fingers, a carefully cultivated sinister expression suggested the deadly pictures they had been shown at the base. "And you won't be wearing one of these," he plucked at his upper layer of furs. "Thermo suit will keep you alive just long enough to load-hop at each point, you work on the double and your driver is kind hearted. Now, let's see you load."

There was a pile of boxes and duffel bags waiting, and a gaping hole in the jumper's middle in which to stow them. Joktar went to work. Most of the cargo was easy enough to handle. But he sweated over the last box and the guard grinned.

"Not riding your tail flames so high now, are you,

fighting man? Wait 'til you have to wrestle that one out at the Halfway Point. We'll have you babbling before you get in.''

Joktar finished the job and the man waved him inside with the cargo.

''Stow in, we're going to run now.''

The door of the cargo space slammed shut, and the new load-hop hurriedly hunted for anchorage in the dark as the jumper pulsed for a take-off. He discovered that the machine had been well named, since the progress of the vehicle alternated unevenly between straightforward rumbling on the surface and sudden blind leaps, shaking the passenger painfully back and forth with the cargo.

In this hold the atmosphere was distinctly colder. Joktar felt his thermo suit adjusting, but not enough to compensate entirely for that drop. But he was not really uncomfortable. And at last the jumper ground to halt.

''Get to it! Dump everything marked in red. Make any mistakes and you'll put 'em back in, slow time!''

The hold door was open and Joktar edged out to be faced by a gust of ice feathered wind. He gasped and choked, then he could breathe again, and shouldered out the first bag. A furred guard, masked, stood with a drawn blaster to one side.

Only that blaster was not on the load-hop, Joktar learned in one quick glance. Rather, the stance of the company man suggested trouble from beyond, where a swirling curtain of fine snow and ice crystals made a moving mist.

Joktar sprinted past the guard, dumped the bag at

the side of a small dome and made a second lunge with a box. A pair of smaller bags, and then he could spot no more red marks. He thumped on the roof of the hold and the door closed. The machine rumbled on. Joktar breathed on his hands. He had stripped off his thermo mitts to find that his fingers were stiff, but not numb.

He began to wonder about the jumper. There was a driver somewhere aloft, and very probably a guard. Two men at least and both armed. He was unarmed and locked in between halts. He eyed the cargo about him speculatively. Could the contents of any of these boxes and bags serve his purpose? He investigated, only to discover that with bare hands none of the containers could be forced. Naturally! Who would leave a slave shut in with the raw materials for rebellion?

He'd either have to move during an unloading period, or just wait for some lucky chance. As a gambler he knew the odd pattern of percentages which his kind generally termed luck. There were men, he had seen them in action, who had times when they could call the sequence of cards and be sure they were right. That was a self-confidence he himself had known at intervals. But one could not control that ability at will.

Only could he afford to wait for one of those mysterious waves of luck, hoping to ride to freedom on its crest? He continued to rub his hands together as if limbering his fingers for a very important deal.

The jumper was climbing, her next port of call must be high in the mountains. According to what he had heard at Siwaki, the "holes" of the explorer-prospectors were always in danger. A company man had to be highly paid to venture that far from the safety of the main road and the mine settlement. How many men manned a hole, and how long did each party stay in such isolation? Did they use E labor? To escape from such an outpost must be easier than from the compounds at the mines.

The jumper was slowing down. Another post? No, the machine was reversing.

But not quickly enough!

A hammer blow struck the front end and the vehicle's backward spurt slowed to a feeble crawl. The floor under Joktar tilted at a sharp angle, the crawl became a skid. He tried to dodge the shifting cargo. Then the pace of the skid was fantastically accelerated. His last conscious thought was that the driver had lost control and they were falling down some mountain slope.

Joktar stirred feebly. No light now . . . dark and cold, such cold as he had never before known. He pushed against the obstruction pinning him down, felt a package give until he was able to free his legs. No bones broken; but his body was stiff and bruised.

The jumper was silent, no throb of motor. And the heat of the cargo hold had seeped away. He pounded on the wall in a sudden spurt of panic. There was no answer, just as somehow he had known there would not be. But he must get out of this trap.

Perhaps the machine had been rigged with an emergency exit in expectation of just such an accident. His exploration, conducted by touch, brought him to a panel which yielded. Pushing that up he forced an opening for escape.

4

SNOW CASCADED through the opening to engulf him. Now he could hear the scream of wind through the broken fangs of the peaks, a shriek of ravening hunger. He fought the snow with his hands, kicked his way out, until he sat on the side of the half-buried jumper.

It had been evening when he loaded that machine back at the road station. Now the sky was gray, he judged the hour early morning. The jumper had been jammed by a slide into a narrow valley, he could sight the scars of its passage down the mountain.

Joktar set to work digging, laboring to uncover the driver's compartment. A half hour later, breathing hard, he had that wreckage clear. The driver and the guard might have died before the fall, for it was plain from the evidence that the jumper had been first smashed by the wing of an avalanche. From the dead he must take the means of keeping himself alive.

The sun was up, awaking glitter on the snow field,

when Joktar inventoried his new wealth, reckoning his supplies as weapons in his fight for survival and freedom.

Over his thermo suit he now wore furs, the coat a little large, as were the warmly lined boots that reached to midthigh. The driver's blaster had been crushed, but the guard's weapon was now belted around him. He had found the emergency rations, eaten a full meal. And now he set about making up a pack of necessities, a force axe, food, a map ripped from the stereo-case of the vehicle.

Among the cargo there must be other things he could use, but the amount he could pack was strictly limited. Maybe, after he explored and found a base to hole up in, he could return and loot again, if the rescue force from the company had not located the wreck.

Joktar's efforts had kept his mind fully occupied. Only when he had his pack assembled and stood up to search for the best path out of the valley did the full force of his present loneliness strike. In spite of his lack of any close friends on the streets, Joktar had never before been totally removed from the physical presence of human beings. In the pens of the E-station, aboard the jumper, there had always been others, even if he had known them to be inimical.

Now he stood alone, buffeted by a moaning wind. To hunt out his own kind was to choose to return to the very imprisonment he fled. He had to face this as he had always faced any danger, with a core of stubborn determination based upon every ounce of will. With Fenris' wolf's breath at his back, he plunged into the drifts of the valley.

But he was not through the end notch before he

began to doubt the wisdom of his course. The sun, shining when he left the wreck, was covered now by a mass of clouds, driving the darkness of twilight down upon the half-buried landscape. Storm! And the horror stories of the port were warning that he must find shelter.

Joktar rounded a mass of boulders imbedded in frozen earth and snow, the debris of an earlier avalanche. Something now showed through the murk, a line of smoke whipped by the wind. His mittened hand went to his blaster, holding the weapon against the thick fur of his new coat. Did that smoke mark another hole? But he was no longer unarmed, and he had to find cover. Joktar floundered on towards that tenuous beacon.

Only no dome showed above the drifts, nothing to suggest any human camp site. And the wind puffed to him a smell ripe with rottenness, that lacerated the inner lining of his nostrils and throat. Joktar retched and coughed. Some of that reek had been filtered by his face mask, but he was still sickened by it.

Now he knew how wrong he had been in his guess about the smoke's source. Instead of a human outpost, he had been steadily approaching one of the major perils of Fenris, a poisonous hot spring where the melting snow seeped through porous rock, to issue forth again as lethal steam. Men and animals, trapped in such country while seeking warmth ended as piles of bones to warn off their kind.

Joktar collapsed in the snow as another coughing bout racked him. He tore off his mask, rubbed the white stuff he snatched up in both hands across his gasping mouth. Still on his hands and knees he crawled away from that whipping banner of steam,

45

ploughing head first into a mat of sponge-like brush, the very impetus of his charge carrying him over the initial rubbery resistance.

So he tumbled head first into a deep crease in the floor of the valley. Brush snapped back over his head, roofing out the snow and most of the fury of the wind. After some moments he realized that by blind chance alone he had found the shelter he needed as the storm hit with a hammer blow.

The wild rage overhead was deafening, beating out coherent thought, the power to do anything except endure for the length of the fury. Joktar squirmed against the hard earth, drew up his legs and arms into the loose folds of his outer furs, rolling ball-wise. The shriek of the wind began a throb in his head, a beat in his blood. This was beyond anything he had ever known, and at last he retreated numbly into unconsciousness.

His rousing was as dazed as the process of revival at the port. He stretched cramped limbs, felt the pain of renewed circulation. And he had no idea that he was the first man since the Terrans had landed on Fenris to survive a blanket storm in the open. A subconscious will to live continued to direct his struggles. In spite of the brush roof a quantity of snow had drifted around him and he beat free of this covering.

Sitting up in the hollow the twisting and turning of his body had made, Joktar fumbled with his pack, found food in the form of a self-heating can of stew. The top fell from his shaking fingers, some of the contents slopped across the back of his hand. But he ate, and the warmth of that specially prepared nourishment soothed mouth and throat, gathered comfortably in his middle. He had resolution enough to cap the container before he finished the ration. Then, as he chewed on a wafer of concentrates, he hunted for a thin section in the brush wall. The howl of the wind had died, only the rustle of his furs, and the creak of snow under him could be heard.

To break through the brush was so difficult he was tempted to use his blaster as a cutter. Only the knowledge that he did not have an extra charge was a deterrent, and the same was true for the force axe which must provide him with a reserve weapon. A last bull's rush, his arms protectingly over his face, carried him out.

Overhead the sky was gray, but there were no thick clouds. He could see with sharp clarity the barriers of cliff walls making a girdle about the valley. Believing it must be close to evening he began a hunt for better shelter.

Underfoot the snow creaked. The eerie stillness was somehow more nerve twisting than the onslaught of the storm. He was one small living thing in that white cup where only the poisonous flag of steam waved. And that quiet brought down on him once more the sensation of loneliness. Were there no birds, no animals, nothing else alive here?

The temptation to return to the wreck pulled at him so strongly that he started back. As he gained the foot of the break leading into the smaller valley sound rent the air, a rumble as of thunder, magnified and echoed from the peaks.

Out of the narrow cut he had been about to enter, puffed a cloud of white as the roar died away. Avalanche! Another snow slide that built in seconds a wall between him and the jumper.

Shaking his head dazedly, Joktar retreated down valley, no goal in mind now. There was the brush masked cut, but he wanted no more of that. His head ached, his snow-caked boots and coat weighed him down. He headed for the cliff to his left.

Another rumble back in the peaks. Tons of snow and earth must have cascaded down that time. Perhaps the jumper was now completely buried. He was sobbing a little as he wavered along, reeling against a pinnacle of rock half detached from the parent cliff. Steadying himself with one hand, Joktar blinked at what that stone sentry guarded, a black break in the wall. Maybe it was a cave!

The Terran lurched toward the pocket of dark, his free hand out to it in a gesture close to supplication, his other gripping the blaster. And because he had that weapon ready, he did not die.

For, without any sound of warning, hideous death launched from the cave, aiming for his head and shoulders. Sheer instinct brought the barrel of his blaster up, set his finger to the firing button, as a slavering weight bowled him back through a crusted reef of snow.

Claws caught and tore with convulsive jerks at the loose folds of fur, and the excess material protecting his body. For the thing which attacked him was dead before they hit the ground together, the stench of its burned fur and scorched flesh marking the success of his blaster bolt. He lay under the weight of the beast, too shaken to struggle free, hardly daring to believe that he was not seriously injured.

When he did throw off the mangled carcass he

examined it. This was no "lamby," the evil tempered ruminant which was certainly no "lamb" to its
hunters, though its fine, velvety fur with the tightly
curled overcoat was accepted as legal tender on
Fenris. This fur was not lamby; where it was still
unblackened, it was white with an undercoat of faint
blue, a perfect match in shade to the snow drifts.
There were no hooves, but large paws on all four
limbs, which were heavily furred and had retractable
claws. The width of those feet suggested their owner
could prowl over crusts that another might break
through. The head was wide, showing a double row
of fangs; the mark of a meat eater. And above that
blunt muzzle were set two over-sized eyes which
Joktar studied closely.

They did not resemble any proper animal eyes he
had known, for the balls were collections of myriad
lenses, each equipped with a minute lid of its own;
some were now closed, others wide open, as if the
beast could use all or just a fraction of its seeing
apparatus, as it pleased. And in contrast to the size of
the eyes, the ears were unusually small and well
hidden in the thick fur. A cat, or a bear? Anyway it
was sudden death on four feet.

Joktar stood up, trying to pull his tattered fur coat
into place. The rank smell of the creature filled the
air. With caution he approached the hole from which
it had sprung to attack. Dropping to one knee, he
snapped the blaster on to a wave pattern and aimed it
into the cave. There was an answering puff of fire,
from the bedding of the beast he discovered when he
at last crawled in to kick out the noisome smoldering
mass.

Using his belt knife he tore at the brush for fire

wood, dragging a mound of the stuff back to the cave. The scorched smell still hung about the stiffening carcass of the cat-bear, but now he no longer found that odor revolting. Instead he turned upon the body, knife in hand.

Hacking off the loose hide he found a layer of yellow fat and haggled that free in chunks, his untutored butchery a messy job. But Joktar got what he wanted, fresh meat, which appealed to him more than the concentrates and scientifically balanced rations of the emergency supplies.

The chunks of meat he spitted and tried to roast were charred rather than cooked, but he chewed them down avidly. The animal's fat answered some inner craving and he gorged on it. Washing his hands and face with snow, he huddled back into the cave to total up assets and debits with the cool caution born of his past employment at the gaming tables.

He was alive, in spite of some narrow escapes. He was armed, though he would have to conserve the voltage clip of the blaster. There were the supplies he had looted from the jumper. Also, the map.

Joktar unfolded that in the flickering light of the fire. The thick mark, curling between wavering lines which must represent mountains, could be the road from the space port to the mines. And the smaller, dotted lines should be trails to the holes. A red cross on one suggested it was the outpost where he had unloaded cargo. But he could not be sure. There was a second red cross, only they had never reached this second stop on their trip. Perhaps somewhere between those two marks the jumper had gone over the cliff. He shrugged, this was all just guessing.

The glaring truth which he had to face was that there could be no shelter on Fenris for off-worlders except at the port or the mines. And if he ventured into either he would betray himself. Yet he was also sure he could not continue to live off the country.

Suppose he struck due west to the main road. But, he could only follow that to Siwaki and there a newcomer in a small community would be a marked man. The port, the mines, the road stations—all traps for the escapee. But what about the prospectors' holes? He was handicapped by his lack of knowledge. How many men to a hole? How often were they visited by supply jumpers? What form of communication with the mines did they have? And could he even hope to locate one of them in this white wilderness?

As he curled up behind his barrier of fire Joktar knew a certain renewal of confidence, perhaps induced by his full stomach and the fact that so far he had managed to beat the odds. There was tomorrow in which to act, and he was still alive.

The night was not quiet, for the half-butchered carcass proved bait for other inhabitants of Fenris. There were weird cries of protest and warning, snarls of battle, eyes gleaming across the flames at him. At last he sat up, blaster on his knee, straining his eyes in an effort to make out the forms he sensed waited out there for his fire to die.

When the morning dawned the calm held, not even a cat's-paw of wind dabbed across the snow dunes. Joktar shrugged on his pack and tried to pick out a goal. The jumper lay to the north, at least he believed that the choked valley which held its wreckage lay to the north. He began to walk in that direction.

The banners of poisonous steam ascended unruffled, marking a stretch of bare rock mottled with yellowish encrustations. But his path away from there was not easy. The snow had been sculptured into banks as desert sand is driven into dunes, each bank given a knife-sharp coating. To venture would leave him thigh or waist deep in soft snow. So he wove a trail back and forth.

In all the white immensity he was the only moving creature. No bird quartered the sky, and if any animal skulked there, Joktar could not spot it. Loneliness ate into him and he redoubled his struggles to reach the cliffs. Right beyond a single barrier might lie the road which the jumper had traveled.

He paused, fought for control. To venture further down that path of thought was to end pounding at the door of some mine dome begging to be taken into its slave gang! More than just the active horrors the emigrants had been shown at the port might keep a man fast in bondage, the stark emptiness of Fenris itself worked for the companies.

Joktar reached the cliffs, squatted in the lee of a boulder to eat of the fat he had seared in his morning fire; he followed those greasy mouthfuls with a concentrate tablet. Weariness weighed on him like an extra pack on his shoulders, but his determination to keep going set him to climbing.

He dragged himself up on a plateau where the wind had swept away the snow which so encumbered the valley. To reach the other edge of that table land and see the new valley below was relatively easy. There was one thing about this snow-buried country, when the wind was dead there was no way to hide a trail. And below he could see one.

Trees here were much taller than the stunted brush which had sheltered him from the storm. And into a grove of them wound that trail, coming out again and striking off at right angles.

Those tracks drew Joktar. He fought, he crawled, he staggered on until he reached those two smoothly packed strips which hinted at a vehicle of some kind, the spoor running between them which might mark a man's passing. He trailed it among the trees, out into the open, turned northward again toward the crags.

The pale sun was well down, evening was closing in. Joktar tried to quicken pace. The tracks led into another narrow valley. He guessed that he was perilously near the end of his strength. His body ached, his breath came in sharp, panting gasps and the snow slope before him dimmed and brightened in rhythm to the pounding of his heart.

Lurching from side to side, unable to keep his feet, he crashed against a wall, clung there, staring blearily ahead. This trail could have been made anytime since the end of the last storm, the traveler could be a day or more ahead.

Here was no cave, but he hollowed out a small burrow in the shelter of a bush and choked down food. Tonight he must sleep. And once more rolled into a ball, Joktar met the cold and the dark as he had met the fury of the storm.

Sound broke the silence of the mountains. Joktar started up. But that had been no roar of avalanche. He blinked at sun on the snow, stirred sluggishly.

What had awakened him, a man's shout, an animal cry?

He hunted for food, realized that his supplies were now low. The last can of self-heating stew had been finished the night before. Now the trail in the snow was his only hope of being guided to shelter or more food. Once more he shambled into the open, and began to trudge on.

A new fear arose to haunt his mind. What if he were traveling in the wrong direction? Had the traveler been bound the other way? He could not back-track now, only trust that he had chosen rightly. His shamble became a wavering trot. Rounding a bend in the valley wall he came upon the unmistakable evidence of a camp.

The stranger had sheltered better than he, a windbreak of boulders had charred sticks of a fire laid before it. Joktar drew off his mitten, poked his fingers into that ashy pile. One fear dissolved, warmth still clung there. He had a blaster, was equipped to fight for what he had to have. Now all that mattered was catching up with the other.

Doggedly the Terran cut down his pace to preserve his strength. But time wore on and he could see no signs of his gaining on the other. A noon time camp and he squatted in the same spot hours later, wondering if he could make contact before nightfall.

The day was graying into dusk when the valley became a narrow slit, a gate way.

"Arrrh. . . ."

That was certainly no human word, echoing hollowly like a beast's roar between the walls. The sound stopped Joktar short. He reached for his blaster, memories of the cat-bear well to the fore.

54

No animal erupted from a pool of shadow to attack. Instead he caught another noise, the sharp, unforgettable crack of a blaster bolt. Six feet ahead a boulder smoked, the stone blackened by that stroke of man-made lightning.

There was no mistaking the warning in that. Joktar threw himself to the left, skidded painfully across the bare gravel which floored the cut, brought up against the cliff, an altogether too small pile of stones providing him with very inadequate refuge.

"You, get out!"

That voice was certainly human, the words Terran, and the order clear.

But Joktar, instead of obeying, dug his mittens into the gravel and flattened himself as well as he could.

5

"I SAID BLAST out of here, snooper!"

The words boomed from rock to rock, distorted by the walls of the cliffs. They were reinforced by a second bolt from the blaster. Gravel smoked less than a yard away as Joktar tried to claw into the iron hard earth.

He was over the first shock and was thinking fast. Such an ambush suggested that the unseen behind that blaster was expecting trouble. Would a company man on a lawful prospecting trip be so wary?

Those guards on the crawlers and jumpers carried a weight of armament through the wilderness. Were the companies facing some other challenge besides an occasional lamby or cat-bear? He remembered suddenly the man in Siwaki who had bid for him with an offer of lamby skins.

But there was no time to wonder. A third crack of

the blaster delivered a flash almost in his eyes. He was sure he smelt the singe of fur that time. And he knew he was licked. So he made the only move possible.

Joktar stood up, walked out into the main cut of the valley, his hands up, mittened palms out. Before him nothing moved, he could not spot the other's lurking place.

"All right, the deal's yours."

"No deals, snooper. No deals with any company man."

For the first time Joktar remembered that his looted furs must carry, breast and back, the company insignia.

"I'm no company man . . ." his words tripped over each other in his eagerness. "I got this coat from—" But he never had a chance to finish his explanation.

"You're just asking for a burn-down, snooper," commented that echoing voice. "Drop your blaster, toss it over by that red rock and then get back down that valley and *fast!*"

A flick of dazzling light not two inches from his right boot underlined that order. With his hands shaking more from frustrated anger than fear, Joktar unbuckled his weapon belt and tossed it with the still holstered blaster at the red rock. He turned glumly and went back, his face taut and hard. Now he had to outthink the man in ambush, if only to win back the weapon which would mean the difference between life and death in this wilderness.

Not sure whether the other would trail him, Joktar slogged back as far as the point where the stranger had halted that noon. Night was close, he couldn't go any farther. At that moment he ceased to care whether a sharpshooter with a blaster crouched behind every rock, he was done.

But he made an effort to grub up brush for a fire. And when that was kindled he sat, allowing the warmth to seep through his torn furs, and ease a little of the weariness of his body. A drop of moisture on his cheek drew his attention to a drift of fine snow particles. The dead calm which had followed the storm was gone. He could hear the call of the rising wind in the peaks.

So he looked about him for cover. A torch improvised from a twist of brush stems gave him light to survey the cliff. And the wind puffed that flame to display a shadowy pock-mark.

The crevice was round and large enough to allow him to insert two fingers. And that hole was only one in a line marching straight up the rock. Some were mere depressions almost filled with a deposit of wind-blown sand and grit. But Joktar did not think they were natural, the borings were too round, the line too straight. Some intelligent mind had fashioned them, and since the labor had been difficult, the reason behind their borings must have been important.

Save that the holes were in a straight line he might have deemed them an aid to a climber, a primitive ladder. A ladder! Suppose one used rungs planted in each hole, pieces of suitably trimmed wood to be fitted and withdrawn at will.

With such equipment one could reach a secret trail along the heights, paralleling the valley, and such a trail would round that ambush.

Roused out of a lethargy induced by fatigue, Joktar smiled, without any gentleness in that sardonic curve of lip. This suggested escape from the valley appealed strongly. Only there was nothing to do at present but wait out the night. He found a boulder-walled nook and slept in snatches while the wind wailed aloft, the snow shifted down to hide the trail he had traced earlier.

In the next day's light he began his hunt for branches strong enough to serve in such a stair. And by noon he had enough hacked lengths to make his attempt. The light of day had shown him that the procession of holes did not, after all, reach to the top of the cliff, but ended in a shadow line about three-quarters of the way up from the valley floor, a line he would not have otherwise noted. That must mark a hidden ledge, the road he sought.

With the first three of his rungs pounded into the waiting holes, Joktar proceeded to the more delicate task of setting the rest while balanced on precarious support. The business required nerve but he kept to it, testing each wooden spike as well as he could before trusting his weight upon it.

How long he crept up that stone surface, he could never afterwards guess. In the end his groping fingers closed on the edge of the ledge and he heaved up, to lie gasping in a wedge-shaped groove cut back into the cliff.

The wind puffed snow in his face and he licked the moisture from his cracked lips. If he stood there would be no head room in that opening, but he crouched on his hands and knees, to draw up his supply bag, wriggle free and add to his equipment all the spindles he could reach. The force axe was now tied to his belt in place of the missing blaster.

Jerking the pack behind him Joktar crawled along that hidden ledge. Now he could mark the ancient tool signs on the weathered surface of the stone. Someone, with incredible effort, had chiseled out this road, which must be concealed from the valley below. But, as he progressed, his first elation dwindled. He couldn't cover miles on his hands and knees. The original fashioners of this passage had either been dwarfs or the discomfort of four-footed progress had not bothered them.

"Four-footed progress," he repeated aloud.

Terrans had been exploring the galaxy now for little less than three centuries. And on more than one world they had discovered traces of other civilizations, ones which had budded, flowered, and faded all in the far past, until even the lifeforms which had conceived and built them had vanished. Four intelligent alien races had been discovered, two of them humanoid. And the planets which housed those had been quarantined, since none had achieved space flight save in their own systems.

Some explorers believed that once there had been another space-roving breed, and that traces of their far flung empire had been found on widely separated worlds in different systems. The one idea which did register was that the Terrans had come late into an old, old field where life was flickering to extinction, where deserted worlds held only the ancient remains of their former fecundity, and where intelligent life was now the exception rather than the rule.

Joktar had listened to the talk of spacemen for years, had heard queer tales spun by men who had prowled the rim until they had lost touch with their own kind. He had seen video shots of strange buildings on long-dead worlds, with races pictured on the walls, not even vaguely human in appearance.

So here he might be using a road made by "men" who were not akin to his species. That he could accept. But suddenly the wedge opened out, he was able to get to his feet. Making better time, he pushed forward, pausing now and then to glance below for landmarks.

The red rock loomed up at last. And now he crept again, having no desire to alert any sentry. But the narrow throat of the valley spread out into an oval basin where the sun glinted on the mirror of an ice-sheathed lake rimmed by a respectable grove of trees.

Flanking the lake was a mound, surely the work of intelligent beings. And the labor which had gone into its erection was awe-inspiring. Great boulders or blocks of stone, taller than a man, surfaced its sides. Crudely cut but fitted together with an engineer's skill, they rose in graduated tiers of stone slabs, the last row forming a thick wall. It was a crude fort, a place of refuge in a hostile land. And it was very old for the base row of blocks were half buried in a rising tide of soil. Also the place was occupied.

That was smoke, not steam from deadly hot springs, curling up from the scattering of hovels constructed of brush and stone. Joktar could see figures moving about. But, save that they were dressed in the furs of Fenrian winter clothing he could not identify them.

The huts on the mound-fort had nothing in common with the domes of the mining companies. In fact the whole camp appeared an impermanent affair used for the same reason its unknown builders had first intended, a shelter in a hostile country. Were 'copters or sweep ships in use on Fenris, those men could have had no defense against attack. A single spraying of nerve gas, a vibrator stationed overhead and every defender might be shaken loose. But here where there was no air transport they were reasonably safe and Joktar did not doubt now that these were no friends to the companies.

Somewhere on that untidy lump of earth and stone must be the man who had ambushed him. And he wanted his blaster back, as well as to learn the motives which had established such a hideout.

Dusk was drawing in, the red points of fires on the mound promised not only warmth but food, also the presence of Joktar's own kind. Only he believed that to try to climb that artificial hillock would bring a rough and perhaps fatal greeting. He went on along the wedge trail, passing the fort, following the cliff back as the outward curve of the wall widened, hoping to find a place to camp for the night.

The valley was larger than he had thought and he was well away from the vicinity of the mound when he discovered what he was seeking as the trail sloped down into a funnel.

Joktar lay belly down and felt below for what he hoped would be the holes necessary to the climbing pins. There they were! He pressed into service again the handful of pegs he had brought, to dangle from the last of those and drop into a cave slit.

He dared make no fire, and his dreams were haunted with terrifying climbs up walls as blaster bolts spit and crackled about him. He awoke, gasping, crawled to the mouth of the cave to look out upon a clear white night. Fenris' large moon awoke a faint glitter along the ridges of snowbanks and visibility was excellent.

The Terran studied the landscape, marking cover which would take him closer to the fort. If he could reach the grove of trees from here without leaving a betraying track on the snow, he might make the foot of the mound undetected. While he was assessing the possibilities of such a move he heard a sound. Was it the creak of snow crushed by a boot? On the air an indistinguishable murmur of voices. Men were coming towards him.

A black shape emerged from the grove, then turned to call back. Joktar saw, sharply outlined against the snow, a tell-tale silhouette; the fellow was armed with a vorp-rod! Another man, another vorp! These strangers weren't playing. The deadliest weapons known: ones strictly forbidden except to be used by special permission of the patrol. A third and a fourth man, the last dragging a flat sled. And all four of them wore fittings over their boots which enabled them to cross the crusts on the drifts without breaking through.

". . . a good report. . . ."

"Teach 'em to spread those filthy holes of theirs west! Smear off a couple and they'll learn. Those guards aren't going to nose out hunting *us*."

One of the squad laughed. "How true! Roose'll lay a trail after we're through that'll leave 'em pop-eyed before their first rest break. *If* they try to follow it. That trick of his using zazaar paws on his boots is enough to panic those dome hounds. They don't like to get far away from their precious roads anyway.''

''What about the one Merrick discovered coming up the valley?'' The new speaker did not sound as carefree as his companions.

''Merrick is going to gather him in today. He only wanted to let him run a little to soften him up. When he brings that snooper in we'll hear the digger sing some pretty songs before we take the usual steps.''

''I don't see how a stranger got in this far without being spotted.''

''Merrick thinks he's a stray. Perhaps from some jumper caught in the last blanket. If his machine broke down the dim-wit might just be stupid enough to wander about hunting the road again. We'll learn what happened when Merrick produces him.''

''Anyway we've other business now.''

''Sure, a hole to scoop. We ought to hit about dawn. We'll get the diggers out with some wake-up fireworks they'll remember.''

Joktar watched the small party swing to the right, hidden again by trees. He hesitated for a moment and then made a gambler's decision, to move after the raiders into the night.

Well past dawn, Joktar lay on the crest of a crag. Somewhere below him the raiding party was stationed; the light colored furs of their outerwear blending in with the snow. A track pressed by jumper treads formed a half loop about a small dome, the interior sun lamp there was a-wink in the half gloom.

Bit by bit he had built up his own explanation for the excursion he had dogged. The companies on Fenris were not supreme. There existed at least one outlaw organization, able to live off the bleak land and operate in the wilderness, who dared to challenge the monopoly. And who were those outlaws? Escapees from E-gangs, such as himself? That they were Terrans or men of some off-world breed he was certain.

There had been stories told back in the SunSpot of rebels on thinly colonized planets. Some men turned against civilization because they were born wanderers, impatient of any restraint, others were cashiered spacemen, criminals a few jumps ahead of the patrol. Fenris with its largely unexplored wilderness, in spite of its forbidding climate, could offer excellent asylum for such.

Joktar tensed. The raiders had parked their sled just below the crag on which he crouched, and now someone was coming back to it. He squirmed forward. One of the outlaws was shucking off his furs, standing up dressed only in a thermo suit and boots. He unrolled and proceeded to don another fur coat, wrapping a face scarf tightly about chin and mouth before he pulled the hood up over his dark thatch of hair. On the new garment were vividly colored patches of company insignia.

So disguised the raider walked briskly back to the jumper trail. Once out on the road his gait altered, he began to stagger as he circled toward the dome, falling to his knees, struggling up again. Joktar watched the performance critically. The act was good, for all the men in the dome could guess this was the survivor of some road wreck. And from his own position he could see the two vorpmen stationed in concealment on either side of the dome entrance.

The counterfeit wayfarer flopped realistically into a drift and lay there for a long moment before making feeble efforts to rise. He managed that drastic tumble so well that Joktar was certain this was not the first time he had played such a role.

Two men issued from the dome running. They wore thermo suits and boots, but no furs. A raider arose to the left, the fourth man Joktar had not been able to spot. Now he skimmed to the door and whipped inside, slamming the cold lock behind him.

Just as the first of the company men reached the man in the drift, he moved with a quick sidewise flip Joktar recognized. One of his unsuspecting prey went off balance, reeling back into the wet embrace of the drift. The attack startled his companion into a momentary pause.

In the dome lights blinked three times. Now the vorpmen came into the open, the black noses of their weapons trained on the company men.

"Freeze! You've had it, diggers!"

No one argued with a vorp, not if he were sane. While the company men obediently "froze" the raider arose and slapped the evidence of drift-wallowing from his furs.

"Woods beasts!" spat the company man on the ground.

The man he had come to aid laughed. "Want your mouth scrubbed out, little man?" he inquired genially. "You make that sound like a naughty word. We're free Fenris woods runners, and don't forget it." His tone, light on the surface, held a bite.

"Wearing a company coat!" the other refused to be intimidated.

The raider smoothed down his furs with one hand as if admiring their fit.

"Good workmanship," he admired. "I'll send Naolas a micro sometime and tell him so. They do you diggers proud. That's why we come to you for help when we need to stock up on supplies. All right, boys, move in and clean out the place."

The whole party entered the dome, raiders and prisoners together. Joktar came to life. His own target was the sled below. Not that he had any hope of finding a weapon there. But there were several bags on it and he had thoughts of adding to his supplies. Only he was not given time to loot. A man came from the dome and Joktar dropped behind a bush.

Peering through a screen which seemed very tenuous, indeed, he saw that the other had holstered his weapon. Apparently the raider feared no more trouble here. Joktar pulled his feet under him, studied the man and the terrain doubtfully. Before he could slam through the bush, the other, if he were any marksman at all, could easily burn him down. He had only the force axe as a counter. Now he felt the tiny throb in the haft as he pressed the button to release the pure energy which served as a blade.

The man picked up the sled cord, gave a sharp jerk to free the runners from the hold of the snow. He dragged it back to the dome, leaving Joktar bitterly disappointed. Caution, engrained in him during his years on the streets, had won.

Frustrated he watched the man re-enter the dome. To get to the sled now, he would have to cross the open and he was wearing a company coat.

It was then, through the earth under him, that he had advance notice of new arrivals. For a moment he did not connect that faint *thud-thud* with trouble. Then he recalled his own ride in a jumper. The dome was about to have some legitimate visitors and the raiders might well be trapped inside.

Joktar sat back on his heels and stared absently at the structure and the waiting sled. Suppose he was to dash down the road, flag the advancing jumper, and warn its crew? The ignominious defeat of the company men could be turned into a victory. And what might he expect in the way of gratitude from the new victors?

As matters stood he had no cause to favor either party. To reveal himself to the company employees could send him straight back to the labor gangs. On the other hand the outlaws had already taken his blaster and had some rather sinister future plans for him. Perhaps it was to his own advantage just to wait and see if these two parties cancelled each other out. Having so logically and prudently balanced one scheme of action against the other, Joktar went to work to do the direct opposite of what good sense dictated.

6

ALMOST INDEPENDENTLY of his thoughts, Joktar's hands moved, scraping up snow, packing the stuff with his fingers into a tight, hard ball. Joktar, who had never had a normal childhood, was instinctively fashioning a weapon known to Terran children far back into the mists of earth-bound time. He cradled the ball, tossed the sphere from one hand to the other. And then he threw with the skill of a practiced knife man.

The missile smashed against the dome with a crack almost as forceful as a blaster bolt. One of the raiders, complete with vorp, burst from the door, took refuge behind the sled, awaiting action.

Now more than vibration through the ground advertised the coming of the jumper. The crunch of its treads on ice and snow could be heard above the purr of an engine laboring to bore ahead. The man in ambush behind the sled whistled shrilly, and the second vorpman came out, crossed the clearing about the dome in a zig-zag rush. It seemed plain that the raiders were preparing to fight rather than run, a decision which surprised Joktar.

A third outlaw emerged and took cover. To all outward appearances the dome was as always when the jumper crawled into view. In the doorway of the dome stood a waiting figure, blaze of company badge on his chest, as one of the jumper's crew climbed out of the control cabin.

Perhaps the sight of the sled alerted the newcomer. He cried out and his hand went to his blaster. Then he spun around and went down in the snow, picked off by a marksman in hiding. The chain lightning which was a vorp in action raked along the jumper just above ground level, leaving fused metal, turning the machine into scrap. Then the same fire struck across the control cabin fusing in turn a nose gun just sliding out to return fire.

Joktar admired the competence of the raiders. In the few minutes since his ball had struck the dome, they had rendered useless the enemy transportation and added its crew to their bag of prisoners. He waited eagerly for their next move.

The man who had been clipped by the blaster was collected, his partner ordered out of the jumper, both hustled inside the dome. There appeared to be no load-up on this trip. When the vorpmen explored the cargo they brought out two boxes to be dumped on the sled.

Joktar watched the raider in the company coat. The man stood on tiptoe to touch the smear of snow left by the Terran's warning, before he turned to study the landscape, sighting for the probable line of flight. Joktar dropped flat, feeling as if the other could spot him out. Instead they went about the business of looting the dome, adding their choice of goods to the sled.

The sun was well up to a mid-morning position before the job was finished, and the captives were brought out to stand by the impotent jumper. Stripped of their furs the company men were tied to that vehicle, their coats dumped beyond reach. Then the vorpmen turned upon the dome, slicing the surface with the full force of their beams, cutting the tough substance into bits. As the jumper, the hole shelter would have to be written off the company books.

"By rights, diggers," the raid leader's voice carried easily to Joktar, "we ought to blast you. You'd burn us quick enough if the situation were reversed. But we'll give you a chance. Pick yourselves free, and you can slog back to the next hole, if that's still in existence by the time you make it. And you can tell Anson Burg that there won't be any more holes left east of the mountain soon."

There was an inarticulate growl in answer to that. Two of the raiders, flanked by the vorpmen, picked up the draw lines of the sled and headed toward Joktar's hiding place.

He had waited too long to retreat. Now his body, numbed by the cold of which he was not entirely conscious, betrayed him. Trying to slip out of sight, he lurched into brush. Instantly a vorp beam snapped in answer.

The fact that his fur coat was too large saved him,

as it had when he encountered the cat-bear. Dazedly he tumbled backward, aware of a burning agony spreading down his arm and across his chest from a point on his shoulder. He rolled in the snow, striving to ease that fire, and plunged back into empty space.

There was shouting, the crackle of dry brush. Joktar gave a small, animal whimper as the fire in his shoulder blazed, making him sick. He struggled to get to his feet, peering around with misty eyes to find that he was entrapped in a pocket beneath a broken crust of snow.

His left arm, his whole left side was useless. But with his right hand he pawed for the force axe. Overhead a furred arm swept back brush, Joktar, his lips tight against his teeth in a snarl of animal rage, swung up the axe to make a last stand.

"Here he is!"

He brought up the axe another fraction of an inch, caught his breath at the answering flash of pain across his chest. Then he threw the weapon, saw it whirl out, knock the blaster from the other's hand.

Joktar leaned against the wall of the pocket. His groping hand found snow, smeared it across his face, hoping the cold wet would aid him to fight off the waves of weakness which blurred his eyes and pushed him close to a black out.

"Another digger?" The shadow of a vorp barrel fell across his face and body. "Let's get him out for a look."

They got him out right enough. Joktar bit his lips against a scream of pain as they lifted him. But he fought to keep on his feet when he was out of the pocket. One of the men facing him wore the disguise of the company coat, but only his eyes were to be seen between the overhang of hood and the breathing mask.

"No. I don't think he's one of this gang. You'll find his tracks back there. He's been trailing us all along."

"Why?" demanded the vorpman.

"That's what we'll have to find out. We'll take him back with us."

"But—" the protest was interrupted as the leader spoke directly to Joktar.

"Did you throw that ball to warn us?"

"Yes," somehow Joktar got the answer out as he sagged forward to his knees, writhed at the pull of the torn and singed furs across his body as the other caught his coat to keep him from falling back into the snow pocket. That last punishment was too much, he blacked out completely.

He lay on his back and yet his body moved, sometimes with a jerk which racked through his side. He opened his eyes, to discover that he lay on the sled, lashed there with the rest of the cargo.

"Awake, digger?" The shadow of the speaker fell across Joktar's face and he turned his head, to look up at the raider who still wore the company coat.

"I'm not from the mines," he faltered. Somehow it was very important to make that point clear.

"Then you're wearing the wrong coat, digger."

"So are you!" mocked Joktar, the Terran's voice stronger and more steady this time.

"Hmmm . . ." the man broke step and then matched his stride once more to the glide of the sled.

"You one of Skene's crowd? Or Kortoski's? If so, you're way out of your territory."

"I'm out," Joktar said deliberately, "of the cargo hold of a jumper where I was load-hop. I'm an emigrant."

"And what happened to the jumper?" A note in that demanded proof for such a preposterous statement.

"Caught in an avalanche. The driver and guard were both dead when I got out. This coat belonged to the guard."

"Nice story. Since when have they been shipping youngsters out in E-ships?" He reached down to pull Joktar's hood well away from his face, inspecting the other with cold and unbelieving eyes.

"I'm older than I look. And when did the E-men worry about the catch in their nets? Jard-Nedlis bought my time at Siwaki all right."

"If you're talking straight, fella, you've pulled off a neat jump of your own. What planet did you emigrate from?"

Joktar's eyes closed wearily. Talking required more effort than he could now find. "Terra," he answered weakly. His eyes were tightly shut so he could not read the astonishment mirrored in those of his captor.

Then, suddenly it was warm and he no longer rode on the sled. There was artificial light in this place, the glow of an atom bulb. Joktar lay not far from a wall of piled stones slovenly chinked with straggles of moss. And the roof over his head was a mat of brush battened down. He shifted on the pallet, enjoying the warmth, to discover that he could not move his left arm, though the worst of the pain was gone out of his shoulder.

A hand appeared, drew a fur robe back over his bandaged chest. Joktar looked up. No hood or mask hid this man's thin face, and the Terran recognized the badge of that deep brown skin, the brand of deep space worn by the crewmen of star ships. But what was a spaceman doing here?

"They tell me you claim to be from Terra," the stranger said abruptly. "What port, Melwambe? Chein-Ho? Warramura? N'Yok?"

"N'Yok."

"JetTown?" Joktar knew by the faint inflection in that tone that this man must know the streets.

He tested the spaceman's knowledge in turn. "I was a dealer for Kern." Had he ever faced this man across a table at the SunSpot? He didn't think so.

"The SunSpot."

He had been right. This man knew JetTown.

"Star-and-comet, three-worlds-wild, nigs-and naughts."

"Star-and comet."

"Rather young to spread 'em out on that table, weren't you?"

Absurdly irritated, Joktar replied with a heat he instantly regretted. "I've dealt for five years, spacer. And if you know Kern's you know no fumbler could keep a table going for him that long!"

To his surprise the other laughed. "You can always touch a man on the raw when you needle his professional pride," he commented. "Yes, I know Kern's reputation, so I'll concede you were a three-point-down man at the tables. As for your age," he rubbed a thumb back and forth under his lower lip and surveyed Joktar measuringly. "There've always been precocious brats in every business. What's your name, dealer?"

"Joktar."

The thumb was still, the measurement became a fixed stare.

"Just Joktar?" As the other pronounced it the name now had an unfamiliar lilt. "Where did you get a name like that?"

"I don't know. Where did you get yours?"

But the other was smiling again. "Not from the Ffallian, that's certain. Gwyfl sanzu korg a llywun. . . ."

That collection of sounds made no sense, yet their cadence fell into a pattern which pricked at the Terran's mind. Was their meaning behind that wall in his brain where Kern's psych-medic had forever erased his past? Joktar struggled up on his elbow to demand:

"What language is that? What did you say?"

The eagerness went out of the spaceman's face. He was cold-eyed now. "If you don't know, then it means nothing to you. You were picked up on a regular E-raid?"

Disappointed, Joktar nodded as he dropped back on the pallet. Now the interrogator proceeded to draw out of him all the details of his life since he had come out of the deep freeze in Siwaki. When the Terran finished the spaceman shook his head.

"You're covered with luck."

"You believe everything I told you?" mocked Joktar, his patience worn to a very fine thread.

78

The other laughed. "Boy, you couldn't give me a wrong answer if you wanted to. You had a sniff of ver-talk before you came around."

Joktar's good fist clamped on the fur robe over him. "Don't take any chances, do you?" he asked in a voice which was even enough, but his eyes were less well controlled.

"On Fenris, you don't. Not if you want to keep out of the companies' claws. You might have been a plant."

Joktar had to accept the truth of that. But the thought of being drugged before he was questioned rankled.

"Who are you?" he shot back.

"My name's Rysdyke, not that that would mean anything to you."

A spark of anger dictated Joktar's reply.

"Erased the rolls?" he asked casually, watching the other to see if that shot took effect. And he was avenged in measure by seeing a dark stain spread under the other's deep tan. However, if that question had stabbed deep in a hidden tender spot, Rysdyke did not permit the jab to rattle him.

"Erased the rolls," he agreed. Then he stood up. "Get yourself some bunk time. The chief'll be in to see you later."

He turned down the atom lamp and went out. But Joktar did not sleep. Instead he reached back into his memory as far as he could, shuffling and dealing out in patterns all the scraps of recollection, as he might have dealt kas-cards, hoping for a winning hand. Only nothing fell properly into place, there were no brilliants on which to bet.

Dim, very dim, pictures of a big ship. Of a woman who crooned to herself, or spoke to him, urging always that they must take care, that they were in danger, that men in uniform personified that danger.

Men in uniform! What uniform? The police? He had never shrunk from them, just known the wariness of the lawless against the law. Spacemen? He had faced hundreds of them across his table with only a general interest in the yarns they could spin, and a slight contempt for their inept playing of a highly skilled game of chance.

There was the officer in gray, the one who had questioned him at the E-station. Perhaps that sniff of ver-talk had heightened his powers of recall, sparked some hidden memory. Yes, it was a gray tunic he hated. He must fear gray tunics, but why?

If he could only force past that mental curtain the long ago conditioning had left in his mind! Rysdyke must know something. What was so odd about his name? And who were the Ffallian? Who spoke that language which had dripped so liquidly from the spaceman's tongue?

True, most of the men he knew had two names. But on the streets nicknames were accepted; admittedly, Joktar was unlike any other he had ever heard. Joktar . . . Ffallian . . . his thoughts began to spin fantastic patterns as he drifted into sleep.

Rysdyke did not return to the hut for the next two days where Joktar, his disappointment and frustration growing, waited to pin him down for an explanation. His nurse, caring for him brusquely but with some experience, was a taciturn man who commented now and then on the state of the weather and carried with him a none-too-pleasant aroma of half-cured skins. He only became animated when Joktar chanced to mention the cat-bear, and then he would favor his patient with a lecture on the habits and natures of various animals to be found in the Fenrian wilderness, pouring forth a flood of facts the Terran found to be interesting after all.

And the more he heard from Roose, the more Joktar began to realize that his own trek across this territory was in the nature of a fabulous exploit. For someone green to Fenris to survive both blanket storm and an attack from a zazaar was astonishing to Roose.

"You did as good as a regular woods runner, boy," he commented. "You'd be able to run a prime trap line. Wait 'til you get that burn of yours scarred over good and you 'n' me'll head out into the breaks and get us some real hunting."

"But I thought you people were in the business of raiding company holes," Joktar hoped to draw out more information.

"Sure, we do that. But we run fur traps, too. Can't get all the grub and supplies we need raiding. 'Bout a dozen of the fellas have lines out and have regular hunting sections up back . . ." he jerked a thumb toward the forepart of the hut. "The chief, he was a trader, he knows how to sell our stuff to smugglers."

"Thank you for the recommendation, Roose."

Joktar recognized the voice, though he had not seen before the face of the man who now entered the hut. This was the raider who had led the attack on the mine hole wearing the livery of the company.

He was as tall as Roose, having the advantage of

Rysdyke by several inches. But unlike the ursine trapper, this man was slender and moved lithely. Now he squatted down by the Terran's pallet.

"So you plan to hit the hills with Roose?"

"Ah, chief, the kid's good! He'd have to be, or he couldn't get him a zazaar and last out a blanket."

The other nodded. "Exactly, Roose. In fact he's so good he bothers me. But there are a lot of surprises in the universe, and by this time we should be used to bombs out of a blue, yellow, or pink sky. Kauto fflywryl orta. . . ."

Again the words meant nothing, yet pried at Joktar's memory.

"I don't understand. . . ."

The other sighed. "No, you don't. Which is a pity. But maybe time'll solve that problem. You were handy with that snow ball back at the hole. I gather you have a dislike for the companies."

"Wouldn't you, under the circumstances?"

"Maybe. But you could have warned them and been given free status."

"Would I?" Joktar returned dryly.

He answered with a smile. "No, probably not. You've guessed rightly just how far their gratitude would reach."

"I know the streets."

"And you're lucky. About one man in a thousand ever escapes, and out of that number, one in five hundred lasts out his first week of freedom."

"You get your recruits the hard way."

"We have exactly two escaped emigrants in this mob. The rest of us are free trappers and a few who do not explain their past occupations."

82

"But you all hate the companies."

"Not the companies," the other corrected him. "Fenris would be a deserted hell hole without the mines. But we are at war with their methods and their deliberate hogging of this planet. The alibite mines occupy a few pimples on this continent, the companies exploit them and that's that. They will do nothing to build up trade or import any goods save the supplies they themselves need. They won't sell passage on their ships to free men, but they bring in their bonded employees and emigrants they can control utterly. The freeze-out is on and has been for two years. Not a single free trader can get field clearance at Siwaki. No ship save a company one or a patrol cruiser can set down here. They think they have Fenris sewn up tight and they want to keep it that way.

"If free man can establish independent holdings on this world the companies can't hold their emigrant gangs without triple the number of guards they now employ or other expensive safety devices. Now the country itself is a barrier against escape, with settlements it wouldn't be.

"They want alibite only. We want other things. Sure, this climate is grim, almost six months of winter, or what seems winter to Terrans. But second generation settlers from Kanbod, or Nord, or Aesir could live well here. Men can adapt, you're an example."

Of what? Joktar wanted to ask when the chief was hailed from outside the hut.

(Closed com between Kronfeld and Morle)

M: Scouts aren't on to our man. The one who took the disc really thought subject had helped mug his partner. He's shipped out since. Serves in the Third Sector, no contact with critical Fifth in the past. Doesn't know Lennox as far as I can learn. So that angle can be washed out.

K: It's pleasant to be able to eliminate *one* small factor anyway. Did your man get to Kern?

M: We're trying. Kern's a vip on the streets. Even the port authorities are touchy about pushing him.

K: Why was he raided then?

M: Funny thing about that. The word around is that Kern arranged that bit of action himself, to get rid of some underlings he didn't trust. And the E-men exceeded their instructions, making a clean sweep. I know he never intended *our* man to be held and he unpocketed for ten others who were pulled in. Hudd did discover that Kern took in the woman and child. Woman died soon after. She was ill when she arrived. He can now establish that the child was our subject. What about the Fenris angle, any word from there?

K: One of Thom's agents tried to bid him in at the auction, but didn't make it; couldn't press that without blowing his cover. He'll pass the word in the outlands. There's a brawl cooking up there and maybe we can spring them during the trouble. But if our information is correct, this lad can take worse than Fenris and still come up fighting. We have to have him. I'd cheerfully fry those service fanatics if I could get these two hands on them and had a hot enough fire handy.

(Report to home office, Harband Mining Company, Project 65, Fenris)

Prospect Hole, Blue Mountain district destroyed by local outlaw group. Request permission to go all out against these woods runners. May we appeal to the patrol for assistance?

(Reply from home office)

Do nothing. Committee on way to investigate situation. Ramifications reach beyond Fenris. Must be no trouble. Repeat, no trouble while Councilor Cullan is on Loki.

7

"SAMMS IS GOING to move. Since he's had the blast out with Raymark and made himself top man in the Kortoski mob, everything's been quiet. Now he wants a general council."

Joktar stood within the slightly open hut door. The major portion of the men housed on the mound-fort were gathered outside listening to a report from a man dressed in full trail kit.

"His runner's going through the Five Peak district. They want us and Ebers' crowd. Samms aims to make it a bit parley. Swears he has a major chance for all of us now—"

Rysdyke interrupted. "This could be the break we've been waiting for, Hogan. Raymark was no good to deal with, he wanted our sections kept separate so we wouldn't have to share any good loot. Samms may be a different sort."

"Samms and Ebers," the chief repeated thoughtfully. "Well, a meet won't do any harm. We can listen to what they have to offer but we don't have to commit ourselves. That is, if this is on a straight orbit. Suppose we say we'll meet them at the River Island," he glanced at the sky, "and, since the signs look promising for a quiet weather spell, make that three days from now. You can tell that to this runner, Marco. Then you take two of the boys with vorps and full supplies. I just want to make sure that no one is planning an incident."

Several of the listening men grinned wolfishly. Joktar gathered that one's trust in one's fellow men did not spread any further on Fenris than it had in the streets. The company broke apart and only Rysdyke and the chief remained before Joktar's hut.

"What do you make of this?" the ex-spaceman wanted to know.

The other's answer was cryptic. "Perks supported Samms just before he called Raymark out."

"Perks? But he turned yellow-belly, sold out to the companies. He doesn't dare leave the Harband compound, he'd be shot on sight after what happened to his squad in that ambush. Oh, do you think Samms might be following the same flight pattern? That why you sent the vorps ahead?"

"Might be" there was a lazy, teasing note in that answer. "Joktar!" He had not turned his head, but he spoke the eavesdropper's name with certainty. The quasi-prisoner opened the makeshift door of the hut.

"Here's the problem, boy," Hogan continued, "you should know its like from the streets. The

Kortoski mob—they range north of here—had Raymark for their boss. He wasn't too bright when it came to planning capers, but he was a good fighter and had what it took to keep his boys in hand, an old time trapper. Then his mob picked up an escapee last year. He'd had luck about as spectacular as yours. Seems Samms is a third generation Martian colonist and so adapts better to this god-forsaken climate.

"Samms began to pick up a following of his own inside the mob, among them one very bright boy, Perks. Perks had furnished a lot of the brains behind Raymark before then. He can plan but he's no leader, most of the mob hate his guts. Then, about four months ago, Perks apparently got fed up. He and a squad he was leading were captured in a quite obvious trap. And since then Perks has fared well at company hands."

"Sold out his own men!" Rysdyke exploded.

"So it appears. Then, a very short time ago, Samms called Raymark to a blast out. Raymark was erased, and Samms is top man. Now," Hogan glanced at Joktar for the first time, "give me *your* unvarnished appraisal of the situation."

"I'd say Samms was planted."

"Where, by whom, for what?" Hogan inquired in that lazy voice.

"On the surface by the companies, maybe to do just what he did, climb to the top in some mob then to take it out of running, or use it to cut down some of the other independents."

"And Perks?"

"Was his runner."

"But you said 'on the surface,' what could lie under that surface?"

"That Samms is straight and the Perks situation is in reverse. Perks has been planted on the company by Samms. When he's rooted there solid, Samms moves to take over the mob. Maybe Perks got news to him to spark that jump."

Hogan laughed. Rysdyke's scowl faded as he chewed on that.

"So speaks a man who knows the streets. That the way a vip such as Kern would move?"

Joktar shrugged, bit his lip as that gesture pulled his sore shoulder.

"With variations. Both are pretty simple set-ups for a man like Kern." He gave credit where it was due. Kern, the intriguer, had been fascinating to watch in operation, and Kern's plans had always worked with the precision of well-tended machinery.

"Then this hot news Samms wants to share with us—" Rysdyke began.

"Could conceivably be the real goods. So we'll attend Samms' council with our own precautions laid down in advance. My young friend," he spoke again directly to Joktar, "the criminal mind is sometimes a distinct asset. I think you should meet Samms, your private estimation of him and his proposal may be enlightening. Suppose you set yourself to the business of getting on your feet in time to accompany us."

The party which left on the third day was a small, select one. As yet Joktar knew only a small portion of the mob. Most of them had been trappers, individuals who had pioneered in the Fenrian backlands before the companies took over. One or two had been prospectors frozen out by the monopolies. The two major exceptions were Rysdyke, a cashiered spaceman, and the chief, Hogan, who had once been a trader in Siwaki, losing his business when the companies closed the port to free ships.

Now Hogan, Rysdyke, Roose, and another trapper named Tolkus, with Joktar in tow, left for the council. But the Terran believed that others had gone before them more secretly.

The day was a fine one with no wind and Joktar stripped off his face mask, having learned that he could do as well without that added covering. Their trail wove into the grove and the Terran tried to picture this country as it was when the big thaw was in progress. Fenris must be a totally different world then. Another track joined the trail they followed. Roose pointed to it.

"Lamby bull, and big!"

"How long ago?"

The trapper dropped to one knee, inspected the indentations in the snow with his nose only a few inches above the markings.

"Maybe an hour, could be less."

"The boys went along here two hours ago, and they'd keep an eye on their back trail," Rysdyke offered.

But Roose was troubled. "Bull following a man trail, that way means he has a real mad on. Might even have been creased by some soft head who didn't hunt him down for the real kill. Those cracked guards along the road take shots at everything moving, and a lamby can travel pretty far with a crease to stir him up. A wounded bull is a hard risk any way you look at it.''

''Well, you know the drill, Roose, we'll make this your party. And, Tolkus, start weaving. This is no time for any of us to get mixed up with a lamby that wants to chew up a human.''

Roose quickened pace, keeping to the trail. While Tolkus wove a new path first to the right, and then to the left, investigating all thick strands of brush or clumps of trees.

''Why did they ever name those devils 'lambys' in the first place?'' Rysdyke wondered.

''Some one with an infernal sense of humor pulled that,'' Hogan remarked. ''Anything *less* like a lamb would be hard to find. Only maybe it's the texture of the fur which gave them that designation.''

''Just a tourist guide at heart, aren't you?'' Rysdyke laughed, ''not that we ever have any tourists to guide, though I'd like to introduce some of the company vips to a lamby. Those bulls are always mean. You get one really mad and he's going to wipe the earth with you or the nearest thing which looks, smells, and moves like you. A lamby will trail a man for miles, hide in the bush along a path, and spike his horns into the first traveler who passes. And since he makes about as much noise as a feather floating in air, he usually wins the first round. Then, if the traveler has had any companions, the lamby will get his in return.''

''But does that satisfy the first victim?'' asked Joktar. ''Lots of little surprises on this world, aren't there?'' He remembered his own sudden entanglement with the zazaar.

"Quite true," Hogan agreed. "So try always to make your first attack the last and in your own favor. Yes, this is not what you might term a pleasant world for a restful vacation."

"But it could be a half-way decent one for men to live on," the ex-spaceman defended the wasteland.

"To what other end do we labor?" the lazy note was back in Hogan's voice. "Break the companies' hold, free Fenris, then comes the millennium."

Rysdyke laughed half angrily. "Don't you believe in anything?"

"Oh, the power of words is well known. And maybe we can badger the companies into recognizing a few rights besides those they sit upon for themselves. But Fenris will never be a garden spot, and men are never going to quit grabbing all they can reach with their grubby fingers. Sweep away the companies here and the vacuum left will be speedily filled. We'll then have master trappers, big traders crowding in, eating up the smaller men, building a kingdom in their turn. And some day the last lamby will be skinned, the last zazaar tracked and denuded of its pelt. Then new deposits of alibite, or something similar will be located, the companies will come back." He rubbed the back of his hand across his mask. "History will repeat itself. That is what is so fatiguing about history, it's so repetitious. Personalities change, the pattern never. Nothing but the same boring mistakes, rises and falls, catastrophes and achievements, balancing each other without end. If man were offered something else—" Hogan's eyes lifted from the trail, to the sky behind the ragged mountain peaks, "he probably wouldn't dare to take it. No, we'll go on and on in our own twisted way until we're finished like the others before us.''

"Those who built your mound-fort?" asked Joktar.

"Yes. Doubtless that was thrown together by some company who had the blah-blah concession here and was determined to hold it against a band of miserable, dirty outlaws. This is a wolfhead planet, now, and it always has been. The very climate pulls men into its pattern. Whoever did grub up that artificial mountain must have had a major enemy breathing down their necks. The situation must have been the same: greed, defense of one's treasure, probably eventual loss to other and stronger attackers. Ah—''

A crack of sound, carrying sharply through the air, put the three into action before its echoes had died away. Joktar, favoring his tender shoulder, shoved sideways, squatting behind the best protection he could find, a tree bole surrounded by a draggle of underbrush. And Rysdyke and Hogan disappeared so skillfully and completely that they might have been permanently removed from the landscape by one of the primitive atomic explosions of Terra's past.

Joktar had not been provided with a blaster and he was wondering how he was expected to defend himself. There was a wisp of smoke curling into the air from a heat shriveled twig. That bit of branch had caught the outer edge of a blaster beam, and it hung only a pace or so beyond where they would have been in another short moment. Since none of them in the least resembled a lamby bull, there was reason to think they had been selected for elimination. Joktar froze, no use provoking another shot from that hidden marksman.

Was someone in Hogan's own organization getting ambitious, wanting to move up as Samms had done, but not willing to risk the face down of a call out where his chief would have an equal chance? Joktar frowned. This was quite like the streets, treachery against treachery, the most cunning player to sweep the board.

Were Hogan and Rysdyke pinned down now as he was, or using their superior knowledge of woodcraft to scout around behind the man in ambush? He would swear there was nothing moving about.

Snow creaked. Joktar turned his head with infinite stealth, feeling that perhaps the lurking menace might be able to catch the whisper of his hood furs as he moved. But what he saw was not a man.

Matted fur? Hair? Wool? Blue-gray in color, so close in shade to the branches which framed it that the actual outlines were blurred. Sprouting from that mat of hair were two sharp, upward-pointing horns, a third centering a broad toad's snout. And all three of those horns were sticky with red clots, clots which had dribbled down to the fur. A drip of mucous from the nose flaps was also discolored with that tell-tale scarlet. This thing had gored to kill and recently.

The eyes, deep-set in that stained fur, blinked. Joktar pressed against his tree, feeling that trunk had suddenly become transparent.

Again that creak of snow. The head pushed forward, bringing into visibility thickly maned shoulders, forefeet with sharply split hooves as dreadfully bedabbled as the horns. Slowly, with caution but no fear, the lamby bull came out into the open path, head up, nostril flaps open to the full.

Those first few steps brought the beast almost level with Joktar. The Terran expected every second to see that head swing in his direction. And for the first time in his life he knew a wave of the kind of fear which saps wits, weakens muscle, makes a man wait supinely for death. He fought against that as the lamby minced almost delicately past his tree. And he could not at first believe the creature was not hunting him.

There came a rush, but not in his direction. The beast leaped along the trail, making an impetuous dive, carrying on into a brush wall between two trees. Crack of blaster bolt. A thin, high wail which could come from an animal or a man. Another crack of blaster, then an inhuman scream of agony.

The stench of burned flesh and hair hung foul on a rising wind. Joktar pulled away from the tree, stumbled into a run which took him along the lamby's route. Why he was impelled to trace that charge he could not have said. But he knew he would find death before him.

He ploughed through the break in the underbrush to a scene of butchery. The lamby, most of its head charred away, lay on the human body it had been trampling. And working to free the latter were Roose and Hogan. A moment later Rysdyke crashed into the small clearing from the other side.

"Tolkus?"

Hogan caught a fragment of torn hood, tugged at it until the head it had once protected rolled limply to display the features of the dead. To Joktar the man was a stranger.

"Who?" Rysdyke's question was half protest. Roose's breath puffed out in a thin white cloud through his mask.

"Never saw this one before, chief." He shoved at the carcass of the lamby, forcing it off the body. The rent and bloodied fur of the stranger's coat bore no company badge.

"Now I wonder," Hogan considered the corpse impersonally. "Could he have been an envoy from Samms or Ebers? Or is someone in our mob ambitious enough to set up a swap."

"That just isn't so!" Roose spun around in the stained snow to stare indignantly up at his leader. "You know that none of the boys'd stand for a swap on you, chief. Never!"

"So I had thought," Hogan commented lazily. "But there can always be sudden changes in the wind of policy. We, or I, was set up for this one. Whether the lamby was part of the original scheme, an extemporaneous last minute double check which failed, or just a coincidence which worked to save the skins of the righteous, we'll never know. In the meantime, I propose we push the pace a little. It would never do for us to be late to the meeting now."

"No," Rysdyke was breathing a little hard. "I want to see who looks surprised when we do arrive."

"Yes, that point has also occurred to me. Joktar, suppose you carry this." Hogan picked up the blaster which had been the property of the dead sniper and tossed it over.

The rock island Hogan had designated for the meeting proved to be another of the remains left by the forgotten earlier inhabitants of Fenris. Once there had been an island in the middle of a now ice-bound river . . . or perhaps there had only been the projection of a reef. But based on that limited foundation was a circular wall of blocks, fitted together with fine skill, supporting now, well above water level, a hollow cone. Smoke ascended from the broken top of the cone, to be tattered by the wind.

"Somebody's there," Rysdyke observed.

But Roose was more intent upon the mountains beyond and Joktar, ignorant as he was of the Fenrian weather signs, could note those banks of gathering clouds in a thick roll to the northeast.

"Weather's not holding," the trapper pointed to the sky. "There's a blanket building."

"Right," Hogan's voice was clipped, urgent. "Tolkus," he ordered the man who had joined them just as they left the forest clearing, "you circle and warn all our boys. Tell them to hunt shelter— quick!"

"But—" Rysdyke began to protest.

"We're not the only ones to see those clouds," Hogan replied. "No one is going to start trouble with a blanket coming. If we do have to face a show down, the action will come after the storm clouds. And the sooner we all get to cover the better!"

The ice covering the river was patterned with the tracks of men and sleds. The sleds themselves were staked out at a break in the cone wall. Hogan made a sharp turn to the left at the point and Joktar, copying him, found a narrow flight of stairs set in the wall itself, the tread stones projecting only inches. The passage was a funnel and the Terran's imagination provided him with a picture of what would happen should a rock be hurled down that grade to meet upward bound traffic.

"Hulllloo!" Hogan's call, echoing eerily up that stair, announced them and they were met by a dozen or so men. In the cone top there were traces of partitions, remains of small cells about the walls, floored with frozen earth. And in the center space a fire blazed while piles of wood filled several of the wall cells.

Even in the short time it had taken them to cross the river and climb the inner stair the clouds had blotted out most of the daylight, stretching in oily black tongues from the peaks.

"Coming up a regular bury-in," commented one of those awaiting Hogan. His speech was underlined by a blast of wind screaming across the broken top of the cone.

And with the wind came a whirling wall of snow. The men were fast at work. Smaller fires were kindled closer to the over-hang of the outer walls. And with such fires before them and the solid blocks of the ancient stone at their backs, they prepared as best they could to wait out the fury of the blanket.

In the open such a storm could bury the unfortunate. But here the ruins afforded almost as much protection as a company dome. The fire in the center hissed out under a dump of snow. Only the constant roaring of the wind was a growing torment to the ears, making it impossible for a man to hear the voice of even the neighbors he crowded against.

8

JOKTAR LEANED his forehead against his knees. Under and around him he could feel the shudder of the cone. There came a crash to be heard even above the boom of the wind. A portion of the ancient stone work gave, was swept inward. Joktar felt the man beside him stir, hitch away. Under the shrilling of the storm, there sounded a thin screaming. He began to crawl after his neighbor.

The moment they ventured away from the wall, wind and snow lashed. They clawed over one of the small cell partitions, came to the mass of rubble which half buried a man. Together they pulled apart the debris, blinded by snow, deafened by the wind, blundering awkwardly because their sense of touch was numbed. Finally they drew the man free, as he screamed again and went limp.

Somehow they got him back to the wall, to the

warmth of their own share of fire. Joktar, his shoulder aching cruelly, half collapsed against that stone support while his companion tried to aid the injured. Until the storm passed there was little they could do for him.

Time moved by no normal measure. Hours . . . half a day . . . Joktar became aware that there were longer and longer pauses in the blasts overhead, that the snow was allowing a window on the open sky once again. As the storm died, men shook free of small drifts, looked about dazedly, not quite sure they had once more beaten Fenris.

"So Gagly got it," one of the white-powdered figures hunched forward to peer into the face of the man they had dragged from the cave-in.

"Gagly?" Hogan stripped off his mitten to push questing fingers into the throat opening of the other's furs. "Yes, he's gone. You're going to miss Gagly, Samms . . . a pilot . . ."

"So, we'll miss him." Wide shoulders moved under the furs of one of the others in a shrug which was close to perfunctory. Above the scarf mask Samms' eyes were pale and shallow like mirrors to reflect an outside world, rather than reveal the emotions of the man who wore them in his skull.

He turned away from his dead follower to call: "Ebers, over here!"

One of the men brushing snow from his furs, stamping numb feet, raised his head, but made no move to obey that brusque summons.

"Ride out, Samms," his voice was a slow drawl, carrying a measure of authority. "We'll chew out your proposition when we're ready."

Above the face mask those pale gray eyes did not change, but Samms' hand twitched, and was quickly checked. That twitch had been toward his blaster, Joktar had not been alone in noting that. Rysdyke, standing to one side, slid his feet a little apart as if bracing his body before calling for a blast out.

Some time passed before the center fire was rebuilt and they gathered around it to share provisions from their trailbags. They were still eating when the leader of the Kortoski mob arose, strode back and forth in the firelight as if his impatience goaded him into at least that counterfeit of action.

"They've leveled a new landing field in the Harband company," he announced. "Plan to deliver supplies there straight without setting down at Siwaki. Just another move towards closing the regular port entirely. When all the fields are located in company areas, we can never hope to bring free traders in here again."

"And what counter measures do you propose?" That was Hogan sounding disinterested, almost languid. Samms came around quickly as if he had been challenged.

"Not to sit on our tails and wait!"

Joktar, watching narrowly, noting the unchanging shallowness of those gray eyes, revised his first judgment of Samms. On the surface, judged by his speech, his attitude, the outlaw was a hot tempered brawler, ready to use weapon or fist to bull his way to what he wanted. A type readily understood by the trappers he sought to rule.

Only those eyes belied such a first reading. And Joktar chose to believe the eyes. Samms had the subtle signs of a gambler who had long ago graduated from a star-and-comet table to games played without the aid of kas-cards or counters. The Terran longed to know what series of events had brought Samms to Fenris as an emigrant. And he marked the other down as dangerous.

"So you don't believe in waiting," Hogan continued calmly. "May we ask what sort of action you are urging on us?"

"They are going to bring in a private ship on the Harband field. Two company vips, six in the crew. What if they found a reception committee ready to scoop the lot. We could dicker with Harband if we had their vips parked up here."

"How did you comb out this information, Samms?" Ebers' drawl came from the other side of the fire.

"Oh, Samms has his lines of information. Pretty effective they are too, it would seem. Perks is really delivering," Hogan returned.

"Perks was planted," the other agreed readily. "When the time comes he'll give us more help than just information!"

"And just how did Perks make himself so solid with the companies that he can give us all this help? Wasn't he the only survivor of a squad who got theirs on the Lizard Back?"

Hogan answered for Samms. "He was. Too bad, Samms, these awkward questions are bound to be asked. They're doubly awkward for you because that squad were mostly loyal to Raymark, weren't they? How *did* Perks make such a fine impression on his new employers? Use a judicious sellout as an introduction?''

A low mutter ran around the circle, growing to a growl. But Samms showed no signs of discomfiture.

"Perks was jumped. Then he was bright enough to take his chances with a good story when they pulled him in. He had one ready.''

"Always be prepared for capture as well as other eventualities,'' remarked Hogan.

"Now,'' Ebers struck in again, "we are being offered some tempting bait and invited to come close and take a sniff. Three mobs able to take this new field! Expect us to swallow that!''

"I would say that the taking of the field would only be a temporary move,'' Hogan spoke directly to Ebers. "Samms has suggested kidnapping. We scoop up the vips, keep them while we dicker with the company, until Harband and the rest promise us the wherewithal to make life merrier here in the wilderness. That it, Samms?''

"Sure, sure,'' Ebers snarled his interruption. "We button up these vips, Harband yells and the patrol comes running. Those lads could cut us off in the breaks and starve us out. And where could we park the vips to have them ready and yet able to breathe and walk?''

"Yes, another small problem. To establish any kind of a semi-permanent base is to invite immediate investigation from the patrol. Move around and we expose our prisoners to the elements and lose them before we can prove their value.''

"Not if we take them off planet!''

That one sentence from Samms might have been the opening blast of a second blanket the way it silenced his listeners. Joktar caught the new note in the other's voice. Samms was getting close to his serious play now.

Hogan plucked at his mask. "Well, well. Do I detect some thoughts of Councilor Cullan and his visit to Loki?"

Again that tiny movement toward the blaster. All of Samms' impatience could not be an act. And Hogan was deliberately applying pressure.

"What's this Cullan got to do with it? He one of the vips?" Ebers wanted to know.

"At present he's a member of the Supreme Council, and he's anti-company, doesn't believe in the monopolies on frontier planets. He's argued the subject for years, now he's beginning to get backing, big backing. And the vips are worrying. Three years ago there was a serious shake-up in the Colonization Section. A man named Kronfeld got in as one of the project directors. He's no political hack, but came up through the technical side. He's talked Alvarn Thomlistos into supporting some of his ideas. And the Great Thom has established a new foundation, backed by the net profits from the Alban Freight, the Orsfo-Kol Mining Corporation and a few other such organizations."

Joktar was startled. The net profits of the companies Hogan listed were enough to make a man slightly breathless when he tried to reckon the amounts of credits involved.

"I don't think I need point out that the Great Thom has friends on a great many different government

106

levels. So Cullan sat down with Kronfeld and listened, *really* listened, to some truths. With Thom backing the spread of these ideas there's going to be a lot of activity around the galaxy. About two months from now Cullan will be on Loki, gathering material for an assault on the company set-up as it is at present. Suppose a shipload of Harband vips, together with some spokesmen from our own select group, were to land there about the same time. Our arrival couldn't be hushed up so that Cullan wouldn't hear of it, and the subject matter could be just his meat. That is what you have in mind, isn't it, Samms?''

If he were aware Hogan had taken over, Samms made no sign of either recognizing that or admitting defeat now.

''You are correct and amazingly well informed.''

''And with Gagly dead you'll need the services of a pilot. Rysdyke now has the distinction of being the only free one on Fenris. Perhaps you had him in mind all along, Gagly had been out of space for five years. Now . . . when do you suggest we make this try to take over the Harband field?''

''You mean you're willing to go along with this crazy scheme, Hogan?'' Ebers sounded incredulous.

''I think it has a number of possibilities.''

''Enough to get us all killed!'' Ebers shot back. It was Samms who answered that.

''Would you rather rot out here? We have to make some definite move against the companies soon and I don't mean just knocking off a hole in the mountains! We really have to cut into their cruising orbits or we're outclassed and through. The free men on

Fenris either climb to the top now or they cease to be free!''

"He's right, you know, Ebers. We've dragged on here for two years now with a closed port. Our trade's been finished entirely for six months. We're three mobs, and a scattering of loners; we're all that are left. And how many new recruits do you get? Not enough to take the places of the men we lose, let alone build up our strength. I give us just about another six months of this life and we *will* be finished.''

Again the mutter ran about the fire-lit circle. Ebers took up the argument.

"And you think, Hogan," he accented the "you" in a way Joktar guessed was intended to needle Samms, "that this plan does have a chance?"

"Oh, the odds against its success are high enough. But would you rather finish really blasting Harband where it will hurt, or let company guards, bad weather and luck whittle you down to nothing out here? And there is a slim chance we may be able to pull it off. Samms has Perks planted, remember?''

"I dunno," Ebers answered slowly, but his protest was not so sharp.

Samms jerked a thumb at the body rolled against the wall of the cone. "We lost one man here today. You don't know how many more might have been caught in the blanket. Better for a man to go down fighting than this way.''

"I have two raiding parties out, I'll have to recall those. And there are maybe some loners who'd join with us. Roughly, maybe fifty. But I won't take any but volunteers.''

108

"Good enough. And I ought to do as well. You, Samms?"

"Thirty—forty—if I can talk some of the loners in," he spoke absently, as if his mind were on another problem.

"Suppose we capture this ship and Rysdyke is able to fly her off world. Who goes along to meet Cullan? We can't load all our men on board."

"A committee, I'd say," Hogan replied. "The rest of our combined forces should hold the company compound if we're successful. Those who stay can arm some of the emigrants. They may not be of use in the open, but they can help defend the domes."

"For how long would we have to hold the compound?" Ebers wanted to know.

Hogan stood up. "This whole scheme is a matter of its, ands, and buts. But I agree Samms has a point. We'd better risk a big gamble now than drift along as we have been doing. This ship combined with Cullan's visit to Loki furnishes us with a chance. Even if we fail, Harband can't sit on the news of our attack, and rumors alone could make things uncomfortable for the companies."

"A lot of good that would do men already dead," Ebers commented sourly. "Only maybe you're right, this is a chance we won't have again. Sounds like a mighty thin one though."

"History is made up of thin chances which have succeeded." Hogan slung his supply bag over his shoulder. "Has Perks given you any idea, Samms, when we should start moving?"

"Soon. You'd better call in your raiding parties."

"Will do." Hogan, Rysdyke, Roose and Joktar left the cone. When they were across the river and heading to the back trail, Hogan spoke to the Terran.

"What do you think of Samms?"

"Just now he isn't very happy."

"Why?"

"Because you're playing the hand he picked."

Hogan laughed. "Yes, I fear I spoiled his original plan somewhat."

"But you backed him, otherwise Ebers would have walked out!" Rysdyke objected.

"He took over," Joktar corrected. With great daring he added a question of his own. "Are you Cullan's man?"

"You've an active imagination, son," was Hogan's only reply.

Fenris' moon, brighter, yet in its way more cold and stark than Terra's, rode a cloudless sky. Below the fluff of brush on the mountain slopes were the clustered domes of the Harband holdings, covering the mouths of the galleries running back into the mountains. There were lights in those domes, and sweeping spotlights outside to cover the land lying within the sonic barrier. These kept off outlaw and beast alike. To Joktar their own expedition seemed increasingly foolhardy.

Hogan might have been reading his mind when, after rising on one knee to use a pair of vision lenses, he said:

"There's this in our favor, they won't be expecting any attack."

"From what I see, they won't have to. How can

anyone get across those spot paths? And what happens if the sonic barrier isn't cut before we reach it?''

"Ifs, ands, maybes and buts again. Perks is to take the barrier out.''

"And will he?'' queried Rysdyke.

Hogan laughed. "How pessimistic we are tonight. Well, the charge hasn't been sounded as yet. You have a chance to withdraw in good order, heroes.''

"There *is* a ship!'' Rysdyke crowded up closer, his hand reaching past Hogan to point at that slim shape caught momentarily in one of the spots: a silver needle aimed at the cold heavens.

"So that much is true,'' Hogan's glasses were aimed, not at the ship, but at the domes with their wreaths of colored lights.

Another of the mob crawled up under the cover of the brush.

"Jumper on the road,'' he reported. "Our boys in it, they flashed the signal.''

Close to sunset, hours before, the first move in their attack had been made when they overran the nearest road station, the personnel found there were imprisoned, their broadcasting equipment smashed, and a jumper and a crawler seized. The machines were now coming along and if, with their cargos of armed men, they could get through the sonic gates, the forces they carried could hold those entrances open for their fellows.

The smaller vehicle proceeded at the odd leaping gait peculiar to its kind and behind it the crawler emerged from around a bend. Hogan loosened his mask, gave a high carrying whistle. Shadows arose, to flit from cover. Joktar heard that whistle picked up, relayed. A pattern of lights winked on the nearest dome, was answered by a beam from the driver's cabin on the jumper.

"Let's hope," Rysdyke breathed as his shoulder rubbed Joktar's in their forward creep, "that we do have the right recognition signals."

The sonic barrier was invisible. The driver maneuvering the jumper along the rutted road would never know he had crossed it successfully until he reached the domes, or doubled up in agony of wrenched nerves and muscles.

On the jumper surged, rolled, surged again. The machine was in the open and the beam of a spot caught and held it for a moment before flicking on. The crawler trailed. If neither vehicle were expected at the compound, there would be questions and perhaps an alarm. Joktar's fingers tightened on the blaster as he watched that all too slow advance.

The spot was halfway through a sweep across the landing field when its funnel of light jerked skywards.

"That's it!"

Perks' moves were coming on schedule. Now the men in hiding went into action as jumper and crawler halted, discharging their cargos in a boil of outlaws dashing on to the domes. The crackle of blaster fire and the shriller explosion of vorps bolts broke the silence of the night as the weird lightning of blaster fire crossed or met in the air.

Joktar ran forward, part of the first wave headed by Hogan. He saw Roose put on a burst of speed, turn to the right. Rysdyke peeled off after the trapper, and Joktar made a third. There would be a guard on the ship but the crew would normally be quartered at the domes. Whether or not this watchman could close the ship in time depended upon the quality of his vigilance and their own rate of speed. Roose went to one knee, fired, while Rysdyke darted on.

A tracer of fire illuminated for a moment the dark mouth of the hatch in the needle's side. A figure writhed, fell out to the scorched ground beneath. Rysdyke reached the crew ladder, was climbing.

Joktar caught the ladder below the ascending pilot, well aware of what an excellent target he must make against the side of the ship. Rysdyke was in the air lock now, a moment or so later Joktar made the same haven.

The lock was empty. Roose was on the ladder below, the pilot was heading with single minded determination for the control cabin. Joktar came out in a short corridor. His only knowledge of the geography of the ship had been the points drilled into him by Rysdyke back in camp, and the ex-pilot had been only guessing at the type of spacer this might be.

For all they knew, members of the crew might be in any of the closed cabins, but their time table allowed no time now for a search. Roose came through, closed the lock. And that shut out the wild clamor of the fight. Now all they could hear was the soft thud of their boots on the stair treads.

Three levels and then they were in the control cabin. Rysdyke had already seated himself in one of the web slung seats, his fingers flickering from button to lever to stud. Roose wriggled through the well opening of the stair, locked down its cover. Joktar relaxed, they could not be easily routed now and Rysdyke had before him the controls governing the ship.

"About now," Roose caught the back on one of the other seats, "they must be trying to raise Siwaki and the patrol on their dome coms." But he did not seem at all alarmed at that thought.

"The only way they can get at us is to try to fry us out with a cruiser's tail flames," Rysdyke returned. "And they've no reason to make this a suicide mission. Well, here goes for the second step, boys."

9

HE TRIGGERED a last lever. "Now we're in business!"

Joktar hoped that the opposition realized that, that those open ports just above the tail fins had been noted and their threat understood. This ship had been adapted for passenger use from an outer rim scouting craft, and it was still equipped with armament designed to protect explorers landing on newly discovered and perhaps hostile worlds.

"Gonna tickle 'em up now?" Roose asked, highly interested.

"Oh, we'll give 'em a shot, to impress. Joktar, press that white stud . . . the one to the left of the four lever plate."

As the Terran did just that, a vision plate, topping one of the control panels, came to life. Rysdyke gave more instructions and suddenly the domes appeared clearly on that square. Flashes of blaster and vorp fire still rent the night about them.

The pilot read dials, made some minute corrections, and then pressed a button.

In the air, well above the dome bubbles, burst a small core of light, light which spread in waves, shooting skyward in angry brilliance. Both blaster and vorp fire were swallowed up in a poisonous green radiance.

"Quite a show," commented Roose. "Where do you plant the next shot?"

"On the crag, over that way." Again Rysdyke made adjustments and fired.

A second ball of angry green glowed on an outjut of the heights behind the domes. The fire continued as if feeding upon the substance of the rock, waves spreading from it for an area of yards. Then the glow died, and where that outjut had been there was nothing but a softly glowing hole eaten into the mountain's skin, a hole which Joktar knew would go on, deeper and deeper, until the charge of the bolt was completely exhausted.

"Now they *should* have been watching that one!" Roose laughed. "Might even bite into one of their precious mine galleries and bust it wide open." He moved closer to the vision plate. "You know, fellas, that wouldn't be a bad idea, let's just chew their mine to pieces."

"It's a thought," Rysdyke was grinning. "But I'm afraid we'll have to wait and see if they'll tail-up first. That's orders."

Now as the glow of the initial shots faded they

116

could catch sight of blaster explosions once more. But it was very evident that the exchange of small fire was not nearly so spirited.

"Calling ship . . . calling ship . . ." a disembodied, metallic voice startled them. Joktar and Roose put back their blasters, smiling sheepishly at each other, while Rysdyke drew the mike of the com to him.

"Ship here. Who calls?"

"This is Waigh. What are you trying to do, you fool, burn us out?"

"That's up to you, Waigh. The range will be corrected one notch for every two minutes you continue your opposition."

There was a startled and baffled silence, before the dome com called again.

"This is Waigh, Cowan, Waigh! You're on range for the domes!"

"Correction," Rysdyke was plainly enjoying the exchange. "This is not Cowan but Rysdyke, commanding officer, ship. We have taken over in the name of Fenrian Free Men. And I am well aware we are on range for your domes, that is our intention."

"That gives him a tough strip to chew on," Roose remarked. "First time in years anyone's warmed Waigh's tail hot enough to really sting him."

"The blaster fire's stopped." Joktar had been studying the scene on the vision plate.

Rysdyke held the mike closer, counting into it. "Ten, nine, eight, seven, six, five, four, three, correction one notch now being made. We mean what we say, Waigh. One!"

He pressed the firing button. A second flower of light appeared on the rock face of the mountain to spread in ripples.

"If the first one didn't eat into one of their galleries, this one certainly will," Roose observed. "Waigh's as stubborn as a lamby, though."

"He may be the top Harband man on Fenris, but he has some visiting vips in there, remember? Hogan's betting the off-worlders won't take kindly seeing good ore disintegrated."

"Ship, this is Sa Kim," the voice coming from the com was distorted, but still more remote in tone than Waigh's bellow. "I speak for Harband. What are your terms?"

"Contact the Free Men ground force. They're prepared to state terms," Rysdyke answered briskly.

The center dome on the vision plate flashed white. Rysdyke put down the mike.

"Well, our move worked. This Sa Kim is ready to talk."

Roose stretched. "As neat a job as I ever had a hand in. The chief might have been taking company compounds all his life."

Rysdyke stirred. "He might just have to take over more than this compound."

Joktar leaned back, his slung seat swayed a little. "Trouble with Samms?"

"Yes." With an overflow of furs Roose fitted his bulk into another of the cabin seats. "I kinda thought Samms was shaping up into a lord-high-whathaveyou. But, again, he isn't too solid with his own mob. The Perks deal still smells as far as some of the boys are concerned. I'd say if our chief raised his finger and said, 'Boys, I'm taking over, as of here and now,' Samms could only ask for a blast out to settle it. Then he'd have as much chance as a snow ball in a vorp beam. The chief moves slow when he's not being snarled at, but I've seen him take two call outs against top men. He's alive: they aren't.''

"Who *is* Hogan?" Joktar asked impulsively.

Rysdyke's voice was chill. "We don't ask a man here on Fenris what he was off-world. Hogan was a trader in Siwaki. When the trade was pinched off, he turned woods runner.''

"Sure," Roose nodded. "Only me, I don't think he was ever trader, or hunter. He gets a big kick out of blasting the companies where it hurts the most. But he knows a lot about what's going on off-world. You heard how he spouted off at the meeting. I think he's an undercover man for someone big—''

"Ship!"

This time they all recognized the voice. Rysdkye caught for the mike eagerly.

"Ship here."

"This is Hogan. The deal's complete, visitors coming, be ready to open ports.''

"That we will, chief."

Roose sent his seat bobbing with a stir. "Wonder what kind of a deal they made. Might circulate a little and find out.''

"We stick here. Too easy for someone to sneak in and take over, the same way we did." Rysdyke put down the mike.

"When do you take off for Loki?" Roose wanted to know.

119

The pilot shrugged. "It'll have to be soon. Hogan wants to planet before Cullan arrives."

"Loki. Fenris is cold, Hel hot, and Loki bare rock and water. This is a damn twister of a system."

"You chose to come here."

"Sure, but then me, I'm second generation from Westlund. We're used to cold there. It's not as bad as Fenris, but still cold. I came here for the first alibite rush. Staked me a good claim down on the Frater. That was before the companies rigged registration. I was doing pretty good ten years ago, then they started the freeze out. My stamper broke down in a cold clip, couldn't get me a new one through their shipping regulations. So . . ." he spread out his mittened hands, "I lost time on the claim, couldn't deliver my tax quota and they took over. They did the same with all the early boys—those who weren't burned trying to fight it out.

"Well, I'd done some lamby hunting on the side, so I made a fresh start that way, dealing through the chief. When they tried to stamp him flat we both hit the outlands together. I figure the companies owe me about eight years' living. Maybe now I can collect some of that."

"Party coming," Joktar had been watching the plate.

Roose squinted at the view of the outside. "Yeah, the chief's leading them. I'll go down and open the door."

Joktar lay on a narrow bunk, pressure straps anchoring him. The ship strained now to break the planetary bounds of gravity. Had he felt this before?

120

Those hazy memories which could not be recaptured, yet existed far inside his brain, answered yes.

Weight crushed him, lay heavy on his bones, lungs, flesh. He fought back in his own way, striving to relax nerve and muscle. They were heading out from Fenris. Slowly he turned his head to glance at the other occupant of the small cabin.

Hogan lay still, his eyes closed. He must still be anesthetized by the take-off shot. Joktar's private wonder grew. Why hadn't he, himself, succumbed to that anodyne which eased passengers and crew alike, save for the pilot, through the discomfort of the first upward thrust? In these small ships the break shot was mandatory and he had thought it always worked.

The vibrations reaching him through the walls, the bunk on which he lay, the very air of the cabin was not the punishment he had feared, but rather something more—an energizing revitalizer. He was more alert and alive in spite of the pressure than he had ever remembered being before. It was as if this environment was for him the normal and rational one.

As the pressure lessened, he wanted out of the confines of the cabin. He unfastened the buckles of the straps, sat up on the bunk. The magnetic soles of his looted crew boots anchored him. He took four steps out of the cabin to the ladder. There he paused, making a new discovery. This too was familiar, yet he was no spaceman.

Joktar went to the control cabin. Rysdyke half lay, half sat in the pilot's chair, within finger reach of the manual controls. The ship was on auto, but any slip must be instantly rectified by human training and intelligence.

The Terran dropped into the matching seat before the com unit, watching the vision plate. There was Fenris covering three-quarters of the screen, silver, dark blue, as cold to the sight as it was to all the other senses of the men who battled its forbidding land masses. Joktar closed his eyes, reopened them. That blue and silver ball . . . the color was wrong . . . some long repressed memory shouted so vigorously that he stirred uneasily.

"Gold," he murmured, unaware that the spoke aloud, "a golden world . . ."

Rysdyke was relaxed in the embrace of his chair, the strain of take-off beginning to fade from his young-old face.

"A golden world," he repeated softly. "There is one golden world, or so they say. The Ffallian know . . ." Again he slid into that other unknown tongue with its singing lilt, "Ffal, yruktar llyumn, Ris syuarktur mann . . ."

To Joktar the sounds sang, he could almost make sense of them. But because he could not break the barrier within himself, a small spark of rage glowed. He was being deprived of something truly his own, and until he regained that lost treasure he could not live as did other men.

"Who are the Ffallian and where is the golden world?" His demand was as sharp as a blaster bolt.

Rsydyke answered the second part of his question: "Not on any map of ours."

"Why?"

"Because when it was offered to us, we threw it

away. Or rather it was thrown away for us.'' The frustration in Rysdyke's answer matched the bitterness Joktar knew.

"Why?''

"Because,'' the pilot brought his fist down upon the edge of the control panel as if he were beating against a firmly closed door, ''our vips will not admit that we have superiors in space!''

"But the Kandas, the Thas, the Zaft,'' Joktar told the roll of the planet civilizations the Terrans had found, ''none of them have galactic ships, and only the Tlolen are free in their own solar system.''

"Yes, those who are not to our own level, we can acknowledge them,'' Rysdyke sneered. ''But you haven't heard of the Ffallian, have you, nor of the others . . . those who claim the golden world? We knew . . . we in the service. I myself saw a video tape and heard . . .'' his voice softened. ''And I tried to go out there. That's why they blasted me out of space! Proper scouts see nothing, hear nothing, and never tell anything which is not covered by regulations!''

"Scouts?''

"Those in exploration service. But that had its Bluebeard chambers. You stayed in the limits of your assigned sector; some sectors were off limits altogether. I found a beacon on an asteroid. The signal called me in. And I wasn't the first who had answered. There was a scout ship anchored there, an obsolete type. And in it was a message tape; I ran it for reading, against orders. Then I wanted to go, too.''

"To go where?''

"To where the beacon gave a course, as the other scout had before me. Only I'd signaled in when I first found the beacon and the patrol was after me before I could relay to the Others that I was waiting."

"Waiting for what?"

"For those who set the beacon. It was all down there on the tape. We knew of the Ffallian, we'd seen their ships. The patrol had tried to blast them, only they can't touch them. But the Ffallian are only the messengers—guides—the helping hands we slapped away. For learning that, I was cashiered and sent to Hel in a labor battalion. Hogan got me out because he had need for a pilot. I think he was planning to run an old tramp bucket in here for trading. But he knows about the Ffallian, too, and he doesn't believe in the quarantine."

"What about the scout in the ship you found?"

"He was lucky, he went out there. Quite a few scouts have over the years."

"Perhaps they were captured."

"No!" Rysdyke's answer was emphatic. "Those tapes . . . they were the real thing. There's no reason to fear the Ffallian. Why, they've tried over and over to make contact with us peacefully. And one of our scouts came back and he was shot by command of his own officer."

"Why?"

"Because he had been out there, because he could prove it was all true. He was reported on the records as having been killed by the Others. But you can't shut up a whole post personnel and there was talk. Yes, Marson had been with the Ffallian, and the

Others . . . those who roam the stars we have never explored. And he came back.''

''Why?''

''He brought a concrete offer from them.''

''Why don't the services want anything to do with these aliens?''

''Because they are afraid, the vips are anyway. Those others have what we do not—immortality.'' Rysdyke stared at the vision plate as if he saw there something other than the harsh disc of Fenris. ''Mortals and immortals. The mortals fear and hate the Others for the futures we do not have. We made contact years ago and the vips were frightened, frustrated, felt like children trying to be men. They lashed out, killed, withdrew our forces. But the war has been on our side only.''

''Very true. Except that the Others are not immortal.''

Hogan emerged from the stair well. Wearing the tunic of a ship's officer, he had become a man who might pass unnoticed in the trade section of N'Yok itself.

''No, they are not immortal. That is one thing we *have* learned, and the truth has been concealed by those of our kind who must build monsters to hold their own power. The aliens only have a longer life span.''

''But why?''

Hogan dropped into the third seat. ''Oh, it's all of a piece. We made our first contact fifty years ago. Some men had the facts—Morre, Ksanga, Thom (the Great Thom's grandfather), Marson . . .''

"Morre?" repeated Joktar. Morre was long dead, his star empire built upon his personal charm and brilliance had collasped speedily.

"Just so. Morre was a fanatic, a dangerous one. He was outraged by what he learned at the first contact. The superiority upon which his whole nature was secured was threatened. To him the aliens were a horrible threat, not only to mankind at large, but to him personally, which was worse. So he took steps. Reports were faked, distorted. We were told stories, such as Thom was spaced and murdered by the Others. There were atrocity tales spread among the services, if not the public. Morre had the power to do it. Over a period of a very few years he produced the monsters he believed in. And even after his death the faked evidence stood. In his way Morre was a genius, but we have to suffer for his sins."

"So we fought them," Rysdyke's voice was tired and bleak.

"Yes, in a one-sided way. The Ffallian understood. They withdrew for their own safety—which for at least one reason is more precious than we knew until recently. But they never gave up their hope for a meeting between our species and the aliens they represent. They set up beacons, subtly tuned to attract only men with whom they could establish contact. So men did disappear . . . traders, scouts. Only the Ffallian are not *our* problem. We have plans to make for Loki!"

"To meet Cullan . . ."

Hogan sat quietly, there was a peculiar quality to his silence. He was making up his mind, Joktar

126

believed, being hurried into a decision he would have liked to consider more leisurely.

"On the surface Cullan . . ."

"On the surface?" It was Joktar who applied the prod.

"We have Sa and Minta on board. Their proposition is to see Cullan with them. He will stay at the Seven Stars in Nornes. I'll be with them and so will Samms. And we'll all be under surveillance every moment of the time. So we'll keep one line free. You," he turned to Joktar, "are going to have some more trouble with that shoulder of yours. Let's have a look at it now."

Joktar unsealed his tunic and stripped it off. His undershirt followed. As far as he himself could judge the new pink skin looked healthy enough. He would bear a scar but the burn was well on the way to healing and it was only tender now to direct pressure. Hogan inspected the wound frowningly.

"Looks too good," he commented. "But we can touch it up some. And see that you run a temperature. When we set down on Loki you're to be sent to the clinic."

"Why?"

"Because I want one of us in position to move without being tailed. And secondly I want to be sure of keeping you."

Joktar pulled up his shirt. "I'm not likely to try to ship out without papers or credits."

"Ship out, no, *be* shipped out, maybe." Hogan was, he saw, entirely serious.

"You mean the patrol would pick me up as an emigrant escapee?"

"Listen," Hogan stood before him, hands on hips, scowling a little. "If what I think is true you have more than the patrol to fear now, boy."

Rysdyke'e eyes were narrowed, he nodded in agreement.

"But what have I got to do with your quarrel with the companies on Fenris?"

"Fenris! Fenris is the first, but perhaps the least of our objectives. We're snarled up in half a dozen webs, all being spun by some busy spiders working for opposite ends and with the stickiest means they can manufacture out of their devious minds. If we come through the next week or so and take away even one one-hundredth of the stakes on the table, there'll be action to rock more than one system. Freedom for Fenris . . . great nebulae! We're fighting for freedom for a whole species—our own!"

10

HOGAN STOOD looking down at his own hands, broad hands, pale skinned through lack of exposure, but strong and tough. His fingers moved. Almost, Joktar decided, as if he were gathering up a hand of kascards and spreading out those narrow strips to assess their potential value.

"When do we planet?" he asked.

Rysdyke patted the edge of the panel. "With this little beauty . . . a week, space time. She's built for speed and I'll push her."

"A week . . ." Hogan repeated, but his tone suggested that he desired to cut that in half.

"Our passengers happy?"

"They hadn't come out of break-off sleep when I looked in on them," Hogan answered absently. "Sa is the one to watch. Minta's a bull-headed man but Sa's subtle. He gave in at once when we jumped the compound. His retreat is no sure victory for us."

"What about Samms?"

Hogan grinned. "Samms is busy spinning plans, probably damn good ones. Give that boy another five years and a free hand on Fenris, and perhaps even Sa would have second thoughts about backing him."

"Samms wants Fenris."

"Samms is apt to want a lot of things. Whether he'll be moderately successful in getting them is another matter."

Joktar made his first contribution. "He's dangerous."

"You rate him that?" Hogan favored him with full attention. "Now that's interesting. But there's one thing about Samms, his appetite is bigger than his capacity. He may not be far from discovering that himself the hard way. Now, my wounded hero," Hogan's hand closed upon Joktar's fit shoulder, "you are coming with me to begin languishing in your cabin with a serious relapse. And I warn you, this isn't going to be just an act, it will be a very uncomfortable fact!"

There Hogan was correct. Aided by supplies from the ship's dispensary and a proficiency in their use which led Joktar to believe that this was not the first time such a program had been in force, the outlaw leader produced results which were lamentable as far as his victim was concerned. By the time they set down on Loki, Joktar was almost oblivious of everything save his own discomfort. Shortly after Rysdyke had brought them in for a perfect three fin landing, Hogan stood over his bunk to deliver a series of last minute instructions in a voice which pierced all sick self-preoccupation.

"We're taking off now and you're being sent straight to the clinic. They have orders to put you in isolation. Roll with the beam; you'll hear from us later."

So Joktar's first sight of Nornes was necessarily limited as he was bundled out of the ship into an air scooter, and flown across the maze of islands linked together to form the semi-stable base for the major city of Loki. The buildings were all low, not more than four or five stories high, and the sea beat eternally about the scraps of rock they occupied, making a ceaseless murmur which Joktar found lulling once he was established in a room near the top of one of those structures.

He sat up in bed as the door in the opposite wall became a shimmer of force and then snapped out of existence. The medic who entered was the same who had seen him safely installed in that bed only a short time earlier, but this time he moved with a hint of urgency and the face he turned to his patient was sober.

"What's Hogan's game?" The demand held a hint of hostility.

"Game?" repeated Joktar, the fever artifically induced on board ship still slowed his thinking.

"I agreed to take you in," the medic continued. "I didn't agree to stick my neck out for the big brass to take a swing at."

Joktar's incomprehension must have been mirrored on his face, for the medic paused and then laughed, harshly and without humor. "This is a typical Hogan play. Apparently he didn't brief you either. But it begains to look, fella, as if you're playing bait and the trap's about to be sprung before Hogan expects it—the wrong way."

"I don't understand . . ."

The medic produced a capsule. Dropping it into Joktar's hand he ordered: "Bite that and wake up a little. You'll need a clear head."

Joktar bit. The sharp sting of the enclosed drop of liquid spread through his mouth and, in some odd fashion, up into his head, clearing away the haze which had hung a curtain between him and the world.

"You have visitors. The wrong kind, if I'm any judge."

What had gone wrong? The Terran was alerted now with that old uneasy feeling which had preceded terror in the streets. Had controls slipped from Hogan's grasp?

"What visitors?"

There was a sharp buzz. The medic pressed Joktar back into the enfolding embrace of the foam plast bed. Obediently the Terran relaxed, allowed his head to roll to one side in what he hoped was a realistic pose of weakness, watching the door warily through slits beneath drooping eyelids.

Again the shimmer of a force fading. Another medic stood there. And behind him a spaceman, slight, deeply browned, wearing a gray tunic with a constellation badge. The gleam of stars on his shoulders drew Joktar's notice. A sub-sector commander at least!

132

From those stars Joktar's eyes arose to the brown face, to the other's eyes. His shoulder hurt as muscles tensed. He had faced enmity of his own kind before, the dull hatred of the streets, the wild malice of a smoke-drinker on a binge, the stupid but dangerous brutality of a bully. But what he read now was so chilling that his hand moved under the covers in a frantic, subconscious search for a weapon he no longer possessed. The medic standing beside the bed had gripped the Terran's other wrist and that hold tightened in a quick squeeze which could be a warning. He was not facing direct and open anger, but an emotion beyond that; it was cold, lasting, and completely deadly. The spaceman was regarding him as if he were not really human.

"He's the one," the identification was delivered in a monotone. As the officer raised his hand, two more uniformed figures began to move in.

The medic by the bed spoke over his shoulder. "I protest this intrusion. This man is suspected of fungoid fever."

The advance on the bed halted. Fungoid fever was not only highly contagious, it was one of the most terrifying specters of the spaceways.

"This is an isolation ward, preserved by force fields—" the medic continued, and his colleague broke in:

"I have already warned Commander Lennox, sir. He has a Class A warrant."

The medic dropped Joktar's wrist and turned to face the officer squarely.

"I don't care," he paced his words slowly and with emphasis, "if you have the whole patrol below to back you up, Commander. A patient suspected of fungoid is not going to be released from isolation until we are sure, and I have the backing of the Council on that. Shaw,'' he spoke to the other medic, ''take these men down to Unit C and see that each one of them has the full course of preventive shots . . . they've been inside the door. Now get out of here!''

Somehow the force of his authority sent them away and the door shimmered into place. Joktar sat up. The medic rubbed his hand down his face, he was smiling a little.

''That will give them something to think about,'' he commented with satisfaction. ''Preventive shots will busy them for about four hours and they don't dare refuse them. This is only a temporary respite, you know. If you don't produce fungoid patches in ten hours, Lennox can lift you right out of here. We'll have to make some other move before that time limit. Lennox's no fool, he'll have very inch of this building staked out expecting an escape try. Why is he gunning for you?''

''I honestly don't know. As far as I can remember, I never saw him before.'' *But he wears a gray coat,* Joktar's thoughts drummed, *and that gray tunic is trouble for me.* Why? If he only knew why!

''Hogan! I wish that man would do a little straight talking once in a while. This leaving people in the dark makes for complications.''

''Can you get in touch with him?''

''My dear gentlehomo,'' the medic's irritation was rooted in very apparent exasperation, ''I have been trying to reach Hogan for over an hour. He isn't to be found at any of the three contacts he gave me.''

"Picked up?" Joktar asked. Having swept up Hogan, the authorities might now be gathering in all his followers in a general sweep. Though it was difficult to fit Commander Lennox into a routine police roundup.

"No. We would have been warned of that. Meanwhile, we have to think you out of here, and into hiding somewhere else. And with the guards outside that is going to be a star-class problem."

Joktar, his head clear now, was perfectly willing to tackle what seemed to him not unlike setting up a bolt hole from the SunSpot. But time would pressure them and he had no map of the district in his mind. The islands were connected by bridges and these bridges would be discouragingly easy to close.

"Air transport?" he asked and the medic shook his head.

"The scooters are all powered by beam broadcast. They need only snap that off and every machine would be grounded on the nearest landing surface. And that would be one of their first moves."

"Hogan's supposed to be at the Seven Seas. Where is that in relation to this clinic?"

The medic produced a small hand-video cast, centered its beam on the nearest wall. Instantly a small, clear map snapped into view, each detail vivid.

"We're here. The Seven Stars is the plush hostelry for vips, second island to the left and up, that one which is roughly triangular. The building covers almost the whole island, except for a garden strip to the west, makes it easier to guard. It's a full city within itself; they've got shops, cafes, theaters, everything. Most of the visiting vips never leave it until they are ready to return to the space field. A series of conferences can be booked for meetings.''

''Who could get in without any questions?''

''The staff are all recorded on ident tapes. It would require an operation and too long a time to let you impersonate any one of them. Most of the guests are taped, too.''

Joktar was startled. ''With their consent?''

''Oh, most of them agree when it is presented to them as a protective measure. Loki is a central meeting place, not only for this system, but for the planets of Beta Lupi and Alpha Lupi as well. There are some big deals put over under the roof of the Seven Stars and a good many of the visitors are sensitive about personal safety.''

Joktar began to feel at home, the situation was quite like that of the streets.

''So, staff impersonation is out and guests are taped. Wouldn't anyone at all get in without a recorded checking?''

''Patrol and our friends, the scouts.''

''Patrol is out.''

''Yes, with their inner ident we couldn't possibly plant one of those in you. And the first patrolman you met would have you under control when you didn't respond. On the other hand, the scouts aren't so equipped. The only trouble is there are fewer of them and those few are now out for you.''

Joktar got out of bed. He stood before the map, studying, impressing details upon his memory. ''Got any skin dye,'' he held up his too-pale hands.

''That could be the least of your worries. I can't produce a uniform.''

"No. I'll have to handle that. What time is it? And how long until dark?"

"Dark? They'll keep the big light on the islands tonight. You won't have much dark for a cover. What are you going to do?"

Joktar shook his head. "Just give me a plan of this building and some skin stain, that's all I want. What you don't know, you can't spill later under any talk-shot."

"Entirely correct." The medic became all business. "Your force field is sealed to open only to me or my assistant. I'll be back with what you need as soon as I can. Your 'dark' is due in about an hour."

Joktar paced back and forth across the small room. Whatever drug the medic had given him had finished the fever Hogan had earlier induced, and he was fast regaining his strength. Now he was trying to think his way off the island to the Seven Stars. To wear a scout uniform as his means of entrance there was to court trouble, but that was the simplest and quickest answer to his problem. And if the scouts were few, there would be just that many less to threaten his masquerade.

He throttled his impatience until the medic returned and then went to work with swift efficiency. Liquid applied to his face, neck and hands, gave him a brown skin that could not be distinguished from the heavy tan of the spacemen. And the medic had brought, in addition, a drab set of breeches, seal tunic, and soft boots.

"Maintenance man's suit," he informed Joktar. "You can use the grav drop at the end of this corridor

137

straight to the first undersurface level and be in the maintenance quarters.''

Joktar spread out the rough sketch of the clinic the other had supplied.

"How many undersurface levels?" he asked abruptly. Since his mishap on the roofs of JetTown he was inclined to try for escape underground.

"Four. Level one is utilities; level two, staff quarters; level three, records and storage; level four, power."

"Outside entrances to any?"

For the first time since he returned the medic smiled. "You may just have something. Here," he tapped level two, "there was some enlarging done this year and there is a blind corridor going this way," he traced it on the sketch. "They expect to add a half dozen more rooms along there sometimes in the future. I have a small suite there, myself."

"That runs close to the edge of the island."

"Right. That's why they didn't add living space here . . . or here. But this last room on this side is empty and see how it lies in relation to the outside?"

Joktar saw. "It must be almost under the bridge."

"Yes. Now here on level one," he made another quick dab at the sketch, "is stored emergency bore equipment. You find a portable chewer and bring it down to cut through just below the bridge . . . well, that's as safe a path as I can see."

"What about you? They'll know I had inside help."

"What they think and what they can prove may be two different things. For some reason the scouts aren't parading their reason for wanting to pick you up. And the minute you leave here we'll have another patient in this room, one with every symptom of fungoid fever. As even your own mother couldn't recognize you once the swelling starts, they won't be able to prove for several days that he isn't you. And if you can get to Hogan tonight you'll be all right . . . unless he has been picked up. If that has happened you'll have to manage on your own anyway."

The medic snapped the force field button and Joktar went into the hall. The pale green walls were blank, though they must conceal other doors. He found the grav plate at the end of the corridor and pressed the controls to take him to the service level. When he stepped off into another corridor five floors down, he caught the murmur of voices and flattened against the wall to listen intently.

According to the sketch he had a hall, a large room, and another hall, to transverse. Then came a door which could be unlocked by a small cone he cupped in his hand. From the racked equipment on the other side of that, he must take a chewer and with it get down to the next level, through a maze of living quarters, to the room where he could use the stolen machine. So much depended upon how well populated these lower regions were, though the time for the evening meal was close and most of those off duty would be in the dining rooms.

The murmur of voices died, Joktar strode on, halting again just inside the large room. Two chairs were occupied, by a man wearing a drab tunic akin to his own, and a girl. They were intent upon a video screen, a tray of drinks and dishes on a table beside them. Could he cross unnoticed? He must, for by all indications they were settled for some time. The video picture switched to a fantastic display of no-weight ballet and under the floor of the accompanying off-beat rhythm, Joktar forced himself to walk at an ordinary pace to the far door. Once there he glanced back. Neither of the viewers had moved, he was safe so far.

Breathing a little faster he sprinted down the hall to bring up against the door panel he wanted, wasting no time in digging the point of the cone into the lock hole. The panel moved, and he dodged inside.

Racks of machines faced him in bewildering profusion as he hurried along the shelves in search of the one the medic had described. But when he found it he was dismayed. It could be termed portable, but certainly one could not conceal it. And remembering the distance he had to transport it, Joktar was uneasy.

He explored the room, hoping for some inspiration, and so came upon the cart, already hung with a creeper floor polisher and two dust suckers. To unbolt the former required time he hated to spare, but at length he was able to trundle the compact machine back into hiding under one of the shelves and shove the chewer into its place.

Pushing the cart before him, Joktar left the room, relocking the door panel. Now everything depended on whether he could pass through the service and personnel quarters without awaking suspicion. And that was a gamble he had to take. He looked into the lounge once again. The shrill *thump-thump* of the ballet still rang out there. As all devotees of that particular skull-wracking rhythm, the two watchers apparently liked reception at maximum. Joktar had never cared for no-weight ballet, but at the moment he recognized its worth. Masked by the video clamor he got the cart to the other side of the room.

The hall again . . . then the grav plate. He thumped the descent button and sighed. So far, so good. Though he mustn't relax now; there was, still the personnel quarters to be transversed and the chances of meeting others here were ten to one against them.

As the grav plate halted, Joktar tugged the cart forward again. Through the third door, to the left, down a corridor, then straight right o the end and right again. He was sure of his path, if he wasn't sure of having it all to himself. He would simply have to move along it as if he were employed on some legitimate errand and the medic had made a suggestion or two which could help him there.

More voices. He had just time to jerk the cart away from the corridor door when two young men wearing the tunic insignia of junior interns entered. They were arguing some point and the first never noticed Joktar, but the second gave him a glance and then asked:

"Aren't you behind time coming down here now?"

"Yes, gentlehomo. Special job, the aquarium in the sealounge, it is leaking." To his heartfelt relief it looked as if that excuse was going to get by.

"That thing's been cracked for a week *now* they

141

send someone to look at it!'' grumbled the other intern.

Joktar shoved the cart through the door, allowing himself the faster pace of a man on his way to deal with a leaking aquarium.

11

JOKTAR hunched over the cart, trotting, dreading a challenge, already half able to feel the sizzling agony of a blaster bolt against the area of skin above his midspine. Yard by yard he won his way past closed doors, half open doors, doors from which came the sound of voices, of laughter, of music, of video casts. If the personnel had been summoned to an evening meal either most of the inhabitants of his level were dilatory or they disliked the food.

He made the first turn and saw two more open doors to pass. Now he could no longer give his repair excuse, for the lounge lay in the opposite direction. Exerting a force of will which left him almost physically weak, the Terran kept to an even pace.

Another corridor end, now into the last turn of all. Before him all the doors were closed. This was the newly opened section and there was only one permanent resident, the medic who had given him his directions. He had only to reach the last room and turn the chewer loose on its wall.

Joktar bolted, slamming the cart ahead of him. The door resisted and Joktar pounded until the latch gave stiffly. He wheeled the cart inside the bare room and leaned against the wall, his eyes already seeking the most likely spot on which to work with the chewer.

With the door panel closed, the cart wedged against it as an additional safeguard, Joktar unloaded the machine, turning its dial to the highest frequency. He centered the blunt nose on the point he had selected and pressed the button.

Its low wailing whine tormented the ears; its vibration jarred through his body and set his half-healed shoulder to throbbing. On the wall there was a point of white light. Joktar closed his eyes against the glare, stiffened his body against the beat of the machine. Warmth grew, feeding back to his middle, spreading upward to his shoulders, down his thighs. The warmth was becoming heat, punishing heat. He held fast as that heat scorched until he could smell the fabric of his tunic charring. When he could stand it no longer he leaped back, raised his finger from the control button.

Safe in a far corner of the room Joktar dared to open his eyes. The white sore of eating energy was dulled, but around it rock crumbled. As he blinked against the tears in his eyes, he saw a piece of the wall disappear outward. He turned, loosed the cart, and, with all his strength, rammed it against the broken wall.

There was a moment of resistance before the corrosion of the chewer prevailed and the cart pierced into the open. Joktar jerked it back to use it again and again as a battering ram until he had a hole which was more doorway than window. The roar of surf came from below and a wind carrying the damp of sea spray beat in, dispelling the fumes of the chewer, cooling the rock of the broken wall.

Once more he set the battered cart to act as a door lock before climbing through the hole. Outside, above and slightly to the right was the illuminated line of the bridge link to the next island. The point where he now crouched was well below the ground surface of the clinic island, and Joktar could hear the slap and lick of the waves not too far away. Returning to the cart he unrolled one of the dust sucker hoses. Quickly he fed the line through the hole and then climbed out to use the coil in support.

The rock of the island had not been, as he had feared, smoothed when the buildings were erected. Having hooked himself to the hose with the belt of his tunic, the Terran used his hands to explore. And well within reaching distance he discovered in a promising shadow what he needed—climbing holds. Working his way sidewise he began to climb. He had gained some six feet and the bridge was still several yards above him yet when he was forced to loosen the hose. When it was free the Terran gave the supple length a quick jerk, activating the coiling mechanism to have it withdrawn into the room.

There were no ledges on which he could pause and his muscles ached with strain and tension when he at length swung up on one of the underbraces of the bridge. For a moment he sat astride of a beam, studying the path ahead. To venture up on the surface of that span under the lights was to court instant discovery. His charred, torn clothing and his sudden appearance would be enough to rivet the attention of any guard.

So, if one could not cross on the surface of the bridge, one had to take an under way. And from his present perch that operation did not promise to be easy. Once up on the next island, he must somehow get a scout tunic and then . . . Joktar shook his head. One move at a time, concentrate on what was immediately before him now. His luck had held amazingly and somehow he knew that he *was* riding a gambler's winning streak tonight and that he must push it to the limit.

Water washed high below, beat in white edged lashes on the rocks. And he could not swim. To crawl along the half seen supports before him was going to be an ordeal which would require all his energy and will power. And waiting was not going to make him any more sure-footed. He was past the first fatigue of his climb, it was time to move.

Joktar crept, he edged, twice he swung from one shadowy hold to another. The training he had taken in what now seemed a very distant past came to his aid as his body responded to the demands he made upon it.

There was some traffic on the bridge about him and the vibration carried to him, just as the constant sound of the sea was a warning of menace below. Now and then when he came upon a resting place he paused to wipe his sweating hands on his breeches before making the swing ahead. His world had narrowed to those supports, most of which lay in dangerous pools of shadow.

Time stretched endlessly until his hands fastened in the last hold, and before him again was a rock wall of island. Once up that he would stand again at ground level. He leaned against the wall, forced his breath into a slow and even pattern. Now—

Once more his nails gritted on stone as he groped for finger-holds. Then, long minutes later, he lay belly down on a ledge, backed by a man-made parapet which guarded the approach to the bridge. As Joktar raised to look over that, he saw that the medic had been right in his warning of the extra security Lennox had planted to seal off the clinic. There was the uniform of the local police, also, Joktar's hands caught hard on the parapet, one of the gray-clad scouts, plain under the floodlights.

He watched the conference between the two, hardly daring to hope that the scout was not on regular guard duty. But his luck held. Gray tunic was walking away, heading into the island. Joktar scuttled along his ledge to the end of the parapet. Here were some small ornamental shrubs set out in a fan of soil, a pocket-sized park.

The lights were not the powerful glares of the floods and there were patches of helpful dusk here and there. Once more the Terran followed a well known pattern. Such a stalking game as this was native to the streets. He skulked from one bit of cover to the next, to sprint on into the dark well of a doorway.

So normal was the hum of city noise that he could

blot it from his consciousness, to concentrate on that other sound, the click of the gravity plates on the scout's space boots. So announced, his prey drew opposite the doorway.

With a larger man, or a suspicious one, Joktar might not have had such unqualified success. But the blow delivered in just the right spot, the sweep of arm to bring the limp body in against him, flowed, one into the other, with the timing of an instructor's exhibition. He lowered the unconscius scout to the ground and set about stripping off his uniform. As he sealed the tunic and buckled on the other's blaster belt, he marveled at his own success. This was certainly one of those nights when luck was pouring his way across the table and he couldn't lose even if he wanted to.

The Terran settled the tight gray cap on his head and rolled the unconscious scout into the back of the doorway. Unless the fellow was superhuman he would be out for at least an hour, and groggy for a while afterwards. Wearing Joktar's singed tunic he would have a lot of questions to answer if he were found before he was able to stagger out on his own wobbly feet seeking help.

There were a few other pedestrians on the street, but none near enough to matter. Joktar stepped out of the doorway and began to walk toward the other side of the island and that second bridge which should take him to the Seven Stars, stopping only once by a brightly illuminated shop window to study the identification folder he had taken from his victim.

So, he was Rog Kilinger, detached for special duty with Commander Lennox, perfect! He smiled at

the center display in the window, a collection of
Styrian pearl flowers, their colors flushing faintly
under the pull of the light. The flowers were beauti-
ful. This was a fine night, and Scout Kilinger after
arduous service, doubtless on the barbaric rim, was
entitled to plush relaxation at the Seven Stars. The
best was none too good for brave Rog Kilinger,
Commander Lennox's doughty right, or maybe
lefthand man.

There were police on the second bridge but Joktar's momentary hesitation as he sighted that guard
did not even break his steady gait. Nor did any of the
guards pay him attention until he reached the other
end of the span where the vast pile of the Seven Stars
loomed in a display of lighting and fantastic, scram-
bled architecture from the edge of the sea well into
Loki's sky.

"Ident, gentlehomo?"

With a gesture he hoped careless enough, Joktar
drew out the folder, flipped it open.

"Your business here, scout?"

Joktar grinned. "Just in from the rim, officer,
what do you think?"

The police sentry laughed. "From what I've
heard, scout, you'd better keep off the joy juice.
That commander of yours isn't too easy in judging a
morning-after alibi."

"You got it," Joktar agreed. "But then, what
commander ever is?"

"Lift one for me," the sentry handed back the
case, "it's going to be a long night."

"Something special up?" Joktar made that question as casual as he could.

The sentry shrugged. "Alert B, not that that means much. We get that thrown in our teeth every time a vip has one over five and something leers at him from the vapor shower the next morning. Keep your ident handy, though, they may ask you your name pretty often under a B."

"Thanks for the tip." Joktar sketched a salute and walked on passing from the bridge into the rim of garden beyond. So there was an alert on. But he could not believe that it had been triggered by the discovery of his escape from the clinic. Certainly there would have been a tighter control at the bridge if that were true.

Joktar stepped into the shadow of a fantastically twisted tree and stopped short, watching his back trail. But if anyone had shadowed him from the second island that simplest of checks did not smoke him out. The sounds of music, laughter, and a kind of muted roar issued from the Seven Stars, with the wash of waves making a dull undertone. He could detect no such footfalls as announced the scout.

A party of four gaily dressed couples came out of a flowery clump and ran laughing toward the building. Joktar cut across their path, reached a terrace set with tables, all occupied, and threaded a way between them to the door. Another dining room, and the clothing styles of a dozen planets or systems, a babble of tongues which branched from basic Terran speech to mutate into almost incomprehensible idioms used on the planets of far flung stars.

He looked for a gray tunic to match his own. Saw only one at a far table so he turned in the opposite direction. The smell of good food tickled his nostrils, offered a temptation which was hard to resist. But he kept on toward the next door. And he had almost reached that point when he checked, his startled gaze centering on two men who had just arisen from a small side booth intended for privacy and were now on their way to the same exit he had marked. One of them turned his head a fraction and Joktar knew he was right, Samms!

The Terran rounded a last table, took the two steps up to the door in a quick scramble, and came out, not into a hall or lounge as he had expected, but into a vast bubble which was a city in itself, rising in levels, each crowded with shops, ribboned with move-belts carrying full quotas of passengers, a kaleidoscope of ever moving color in which it would be very easy to lose any quarry.

But Samms' rather drab jacket was the exception in this fashionable world. A glimpse of his wide shoulders drew Joktar into one of the belts and he began moving along it to draw closer to the man from Fenris. Luckily there were other impatient passengers and he did not make himself conspicious by his stalking. And Samms and his diner companion appeared content to allow the belt to transport them at its slower rate. Joktar was close enough to follow them when they did move, leaving the wider belt with a skip for a narrower one winding into a side corridor. There were fewer riders here and Joktar was forced to allow several passengers to get between him and the pair he trailed.

He knew that the party from Fenris had been housed together and he was certain that sooner or later Samms would guide him to their quarters, for he dared not make any enquiry for Hogan. Now Samms' companion stepped courteously aside for a woman and Joktar saw that he was Sa—Sa of Harband! Yet from their attitude one would believe those two ahead to be good friends, rather than enemies who less than three weeks ago had been exchanging blaster shots . . . if not exactly at each other, then by proxy. The old suspicion of Samms' possible double game flowered. And the Terran began to wonder about the wisdom of trailing this ill-assorted pair.

They were leaving the belt, he must make up his mind in a hurry. Joktar, his hand resting near the butt of his blaster, allowed the belt to carry him parallel with the door to the grav-plate shaft where the others now stood, then he jumped off, to come up behind Sa.

Samms glanced around and Joktar expected recognition, but that did not come. For what broke Samms' stolid expression was sharp surprise, a surprise with a touch of wariness in it. And for the first time there was a spark of some emotion in his pale gray eyes.

"What are you doing here?" he demanded. "I told the commander not to move in before nineteen hours."

"The commander likes to take out insurance," Joktar adlibed, "I'm the insurance."

Sa looked over his shoulder. On his thin, well chiseled features there was a distant shadow of annoyance.

"Such last minute additions to well conceived plans," he commented, "always lead to difficulties.

If you go up with us now it will jeopardize our chances of coming to an agreement.''

He had fallen into something, Joktar knew that, though he still could not understand why Samms did not know him. Or did he? Was the outlaw from Fenris doubling on an already muddled trail? But how did the scouts and Lennox come into this?

"I have my orders," he returned shortly.

A grav plate came to a halt before them and the two from Fenris moved on it reluctantly. The Terran guessed that Samms, at least, longed to order him to remain where he was. They arose in a stomach rocking sweep, Samms' inner agitation betrayed by that snap of full power. Joktar braced himself at the hand rail. If they stopped short now. . . .

But Samms slowed the plate and the jar of the halt did not shake them from their footing. In the hall facing them he saw both the green tunic of the planet police and the blue of a patrolman. He waited tensely for Samms to protest to both or either concerning his own presence. But no protest came.

The Fenrian outlaw moved on to the door, placed his palm on its lock, and stepped aside to usher Sa past him. His shoulder half blocked Joktar, but the Terran nudged him on.

They came into a luxurious apartment which now held an odd scene. Hogan and Rysdyke were both stretched out in the soft embrace of eazee-rests. But neither of them were resting easily. A small disc in the hand of a second patrol officer insured that. They were effectively webbed in the bonds of a tangle.

"It would seem," Joktar spoke, "that there's a little trouble here."

The patrolman turned his head to face the muzzle of the scout blaster.

"Pin up!" the Terran snapped.

When he saw the other's finger rise from the disc and Rysdyke and Hogan move, Joktar held out one hand.

"Toss!" he gave his second order, "and make it center!"

The patrolman tossed and the Terran's fingers closed about the tangle control.

"Now, all of you, over there!" His gesture included Samms, Sa, and the patrol officer, sending them to the other side of the room. Holstering his blaster he pushed in the tangle pin.

"You know," he informed them, "there is a way of jamming these so they can't be turned off . . . they have to be burned out. Now I wonder how good my memory is. . . . Sorry." His three captives twisted under a tightening of the coils which held them. And Samms spat a quite exotic suggestion concerning Joktar's past. "There, that ought to do it!" The pin was well wedged to one side and he dropped the tangle to the floor. "Now you'll all stay put until that's burnt out."

Samms made a biting comment concerning Commander Lennox.

"What's Lennox got to do with it?" demanded Rysdyke.

"Yes, that I would like to know. . . . Oh," Hogan laughed, "my good friends have really given themselves away this time, haven't they? They accept the false as readily as the real because they were

154

expecting some such move." His hand dropped on Joktar's shoulder. "How did you manage to arrive like the space marines, all ready for battle in good time?"

Samms' eyes narrowed and he stared at the Terran, for the first time seeing more than the uniform. Again that spark glowed in his eyes. And Joktar knew that Samms would never either forgive or forget this particular meeting.

"The scouts tried to pry me loose from the clinic, I preferred to make the trip under my own power. What I want to know is why?"

"Samms," Hogan reseated himself. "I sadly fear I made a grave error in your case, the error of underestimating you. Lennox got to you, didn't he? I would very much like to know how the commander is so well informed concerning our movements. There has been a bad slip somewhere."

Sa wriggled as if he were trying to find a more easy fit within the invisible ties which held him prisoner.

"Hogan, I am a reasonable individual. You have impressed me that you possess a certain sense of logic; you are able to rise above such dramatics as these, I also believe that Harband is not the primary objective of your present moves. I believe that we may, as you say, be able to make a deal."

Hogan listened with an expression of placid interest. "I am, of course, flattered by your estimate of my character, gentlehomo. Yes, I am attracted to logic, sense, and reason as much as any man. Now, what do you have to offer?"

"Profit . . . and perhaps your life."

Hogan settled closer into the embrace of his chair.

"Both those points are able to hold my full interest, gentlehomo. Will you please turn up your first card?"

12

BEHIND Sa's slender elegance Samms backed the wall. Of the three prisoners Joktar paid him the closest attention. Those shallow eyes were fastened on Hogan and there was an odd deliberation in that gaze. Was his the study of a knife fighter picking out his mark? Samms' control was back, he was assured . . . or waiting. Joktar spoke:

"They're playing for time."

Hogan smiled, answered lazily. "But of course. However, we must preserve the aura of courtesy if not the quality itself. Gentlehomo Sa has not come here to represent anyone but his own company."

Sa nodded his head, his body still held rigid by the grip of the tangle.

"Do you wish me to swear to that on the Truth of the Ancestors?" he inquired with a half sneer.

"Not at all, gentlehomo. I made a statement, I did

not ask for reassurance. Now, what do you have to offer?''

''Suppose the companies relax the import regulations on Fenris, allow free traders to planet?''

''And in return for such a concession?''

''You do not push your case before Cullan.''

''Ah, that's the nip, is it? But I am a little surprised at you, gentlehomo. You immediately offer us what men have died vainly to obtain. And yet you have the reputation of being an astute, sly man. So I shall make some guesses, you need not even signify as to whether I am right or am failing to judge correctly what must be in progress behind several different curtains at this moment.

''First: the companies have been warned their monopolies are in danger. A manifest piece of mismanagement or public scandal now will wreck them and Councilor Cullan is the avowed enemy of their present way of conducting business. In answer to that, gentlehomo, may I say that the end of the companies in their present form, is already upon us. You can not build a dam when a river is in flood. But by granting graciously such concessions as you have already outlined, you might be in a position six months or a year from now, to have the backing of new friends when you need them most. Because the companies are needed on the frontier worlds, but with their policies modified.''

Sa smiled. ''We understand each other perfectly,'' there was almost a note of humor in that. ''May I also point out, gentlehomo, that you are now engaged in a war covering more than one sector. To turn one of your opponents, a minor one that is true, but nevertheless an enemy of sorts, into a neutral or even a friend at this juncture might also divert the tide in your favor.''

''In other words you have information of value.'' Hogan picked up a com mike with attached mirror from the table. ''You have been dealing with Samms, now you offer me certain advantages. Why change? Surely the temporary turning of tables in this room has not had so great an influence . . .''

''You have an argument which counts over this,'' Sa pointed with his chin to the tangle on the floor.

''And that?''

''We do not have time to spare, gentlehomo. An hour ago Lennox thought he had what he wanted. Without that particular advantage on his side the whole government policy, even our way of life, may crack wide open. No, Lennox is not top, you are!''

Hogan held the mirror steady, his face still wore an urban half-smile, but Joktar knew he was on guard.

''Your information sources appear extremely efficient.''

''I assure you that they are, Hogan. And this, too, I will concede, we of the companies must change course or cease to cruise space. You dare not continue to hammer down a cap upon the forces the vips have tried to control. So I tell you, Lennox will move to take back what he wants. He's preparing to move against you tonight.''

There was an odd strangled sound out of Samms. Hogan's finger tapped the code key of the mike. A face flashed on the mirror, its eyes regarded Hogan briefly before it disappeared. Now a code pattern of interwoven light followed. Hogan spoke twice, unknown words, into the mike and the pattern swirled in answer.

"Hogan here, Councilor, we have information that Lennox—"

He did not add another word. He could not. Out of the walls, the floor under them, the very air of the room, the enemy struck.

"Vibrator!" Joktar got that word out, his body twisting involuntarily as he fought against the agonizing pull of the energy beam which must be near, judging by the intensity of its torturing volume.

Rysdyke was already on the floor, writhing, small choking moans being wrung from him as he rolled. Hogan fought, beads of moisture gathering on his forehead, trickling down his flat cheeks. He clutched the mike close to his lips, tried to force out words as his limbs jerked and twitched.

Joktar staggered halfway toward the door panel. The action was like trying to run through thick mud, a mud which in addition sent fiery whips up his body in great stinging cuts. But somehow he kept his feet, was able to take his blaster from the holster and bring its barrel up in line with the door.

An inarticulate cry from Hogan made him look around. The other was signalling with his eyes, demanding. In his hands the mike oscillated back and forth but somehow he made the gesture of holding it out. Joktar stumbled back, to half collapse beside Hogan. His right arm lay across the other's thighs, the blaster held still to face the door.

Then, using all his will power and what remained of his control over his own muscles, Joktar pulled the mike to his mouth. Whether the vibrator had already muted him he did not know, but this was their one chance for help. He worked his lips, trying to conquer their spasmotic fluttering.

"Vi-vibrator here," that was ragged about the edges but the words made sense. If they only did the same for the unseen listener!

There was a ripple of light on the mirror. For one long moment Joktar looked at a face, as the other must sight him. Then the mirror went blank, the hum of an open com died. And the device flew across the room as an involuntary convulsion of Hogan's muscles hurled it.

They must have stepped up the vibrator to the outer limit. Hogan rolled, Rysdyke was drooling blood, and Sa had gone entirely limp, supported by the tangle. While the patrolman was moaning and only half conscious. Of them all Samms clung to some measure of awareness.

And yet, though he was in agony, Joktar could still move. He knew a dim and fleeting wonder at that. The only thing was to use this partial immunity to the utmost. He began to crawl, avoiding Rysdyke, heading for a table he could use as a crutch to regain his feet. He clawed his way up. Before he could again face the door squarely the panel moved.

Hogan lay on the eazee-rest. He was inert, only his eyes still had a small spark of consciousness. Now he made a convulsive struggle to rise as a figure in a protective non-vi suit strode into the room.

Joktar, seeing that suit, knew how pitiful his own hopes of defiance were. A blaster beam, unless snapped up to a concentration which made it dangerous to its user, could make no impression on that kind of armor. Nevertheless the Terran was on his feet and able after a fashion to use a weapon and the stranger in the suit would be expecting no opposition.

The newcomer stooped over Rysdyke, examined him briefly, and kicked him aside, to advance on Hogan. His hand was half raised and flat against the palm Joktar caught the glisten of metal. There were several very small, very deadly arms which could be carried that way. Suddenly he knew that this was not a matter of taking prisoners, but of murder!

There was no way of crossing the space between them in time, not with most of his muscles knotted by the vibrator. But—

Using both hands he swung the blaster around, aimed it, not at the man advancing on Hogan, but at one vital spot on the floor. That crack of bolt was followed by a spurt of white fire leaping from the carpet. Joktar had already lunged forward as men, suddenly released from the destroyed tangle, slumped to the floor, bearing with them the startled stranger.

Joktar lay half across Hogan and his blaster, brought down as a club, had dazed the man in the non-vi suit. But the blow had not landed clean and the other was not stunned as the Terran had gambled. His own reflexes were so slowed by the vibrator that he could not raise his hand in time to ward off a return blow, the force of which sent him rolling to the floor, so weak he could not struggle up again.

He saw that hand sweep up with the bright spark cupped in the palm, swing over him. Then the other paused. Through the transparent face mask his face

wore an expression of complete astonishment. With
his other hand he jerked Joktar into a sitting position,
slammed him back against the eazee-rest and tore
open the front of his tunic. But whatever he sought,
he did not find. Instead he stared at the burn scar on
the Terran's shoulder and his gaze was bleak as his
lips moved, he was speaking into the throat mike of
his suit.

His answer came in the halting of the vibrator
waves. Only none of the men freed from that torture
were able to move and most of them were unconscious. The man in the suit spun Joktar around,
whipped the Terran's limp hands behind him, and
made fast his wrists, before shoving him roughly
back to floor level. So Joktar's attack had been a
forlorn hope after all.

Others were entering the room. Hands on his
shoulders, pulling him up to face the gray-clad man
he had last seen in the clinic. The commander surveyed him coldly, nodded. Joktar looked around.
They were all prisoners, it would seem. Sa, Rysdyke, the patrolman were still out. Of Samms and
Hogan he was not so sure.

Lennox went to the latter. He reached down,
caught a fistful of the trader's hair and pulled his
head around. Hogan's eyes were still open, now his
lips moved in a wry grimace. The commander
smiled thinly.

"This is the end, snooper."

Again Hogan's lips moved without sound. But
Lennox appeared to read some protest.

"We'll take you to headquarters where we know
how to keep mouths shut. I'd like to know how your

employer will keep on with his plans after we finish mopping up. Nobody, *nobody,* you understand," his mouth tightened, the hand entangled in Hogan's hair moved so that the head on which that hair grew, thumped hard against the chair, "nobody makes fools of the scouts! Nor dirties their records, present or past." He looked past Hogan to Joktar with the same deadly coldness he had displayed at the clinic. "We'll run our tests, and if you have found your monster . . . well, he won't survive long! Kelse!" At his call another gray-clad man stepped forward. "The 'copter on the west terrace, see these are loaded in that and get them to headquarters at once."

"You sound in a hurry, Commander."

Bluecoats were pushing aside the gray at the door. Lennox whirled, half crouching, a fighting man ready for an attack. But the man who had spoke wore no weapons, his official cloak, thrown back over one shoulder, had the star within star of the Council, and his face was the one Joktar had last seen on the com mirror.

"This is a service matter, no civil rights, Councilor."

"No civil rights? Yet to my certain knowledge none of these prisoners of yours are enlisted in the scouts. Let me see . . . that is Gentlehome Sa Kim, one of the directors of the Harband Company, and that one is a patrolman. Correct me, of course, if I am not right, Commander, but the patrol is *not* answerable to the scouts, though you are answerable to their admiral. And these here," he glanced at Samms, Hogan and Rysdyke, "are all petitioners in council from Fenris. I was to interview them tomorrow, or rather today, since it is now past midnight. No, you can not in truth claim any of these gentlehomos as members of the scouts, subject to your discipline.''

Lennox's hand shot out, fastened on the collar of Joktar's tunic, dragging him to his wavering feet. ''This one I can and do!''

''So?'' Cullan advanced deliberately across the room, gave Joktar a measuring stare, beginning at his towsled head and descending to his scuffed boots. ''Dober!'' One of the patrolmen at the door came to him. ''Correct me if I am wrong, do the scouts not wear special ident discs at all times!''

''Yes, gentlehomo.''

''Will you please search this man for his disc.''

The patrolman hesitated. Lennox had pulled Joktar half behind him and seemed ready to resist such action.

''Come now, Commander, do not be difficult. If this man is one of yours he will wear such a disc, if he is not and is masquerading as a member of the service, then he has committed an offense which it is my duty as Councilor to investigate.''

Lennox's heavy space tan was darkened by a greenish undercast. He moved with a vast reluctance, and the patrolmen pulled Joktar's tunic half off his shoulders, the undershirt following.

''No disc, gentlehomo,'' he reported woodenly.

''Ah, then, I must be right. This man is an impostor and so will be dealt with along proper channels. I think we must get to the bottom of this whole strange business as soon as possible. Patrolmen, escort all these civilians, and Commander Lennox, to my quarters. You need have no fear concerning escapes, Commander, I have been granted a maximum security apartment. Also medical attention must be provided for those in need of it. We shall assemble later for an informal inquiry.''

At that inquiry, an hour or so later, Joktar occupied a seat he had chosen for himself, the ledge of a window. Behind him the wide sweep of unbreakable op-glass framed the pink-orange of dawn. He raised the cup he balanced between his two hands to his lips and drank. The liquid was cool, but inside him warm, mellow; it was relaxing and renewing. Over the rim of that cup he watched the other occupants of the room with wary intentness.

Rysdyke half reclined in an eazee-rest, the dribble of blood was gone from his chin, but his face was that of a spent runner from whose body the last precious spark of energy had been drawn. And next to him was Samms, far more alert, his flat, silver-plate-like eyes moving slowly from one face to the next. Sa was sipping at a cup, a little shrunken in his finely cut, lusterless silks, but ready. Then a small space and Lennox, Lennox who sat as if he had been forced into that seat by external pressure, held there by a tangle. Beyond Lennox, next to his own perch, Hogan. Only the patrolman was missing from their first company and his place was taken by the strange man wearing the plum tunic of a bureau chief, the man who had tapped Hogan lightly on the shoulder with the familiarity of old camaraderie when he had entered the room minutes earlier, to take his place at Cullan's right, facing the others, and to be introduced as Director Kronfeld.

The Councilor turned his head to the view from the second window behind his chair.

"Dawn," he remarked, "symbolically fitting in a way that we should have a dawn hour for this particular discussion." He picked up a sheet of petition parchment. "I have here a petition in order from a body calling themselves 'Free Men of Fenris,' represented here by Gentlehomos Samms, Rysdyke and Hogan. Do you, Gentlehomo Sa, offer any reasons why the complaint set forth here should not be investigated?"

Sa smiled wearily. "Councilor, one does not win a race by flogging a dead horse. I have already agreed with Gentlehomo Hogan to negotiate terms with those he represents. I can speak only for Harband but—"

"But with their united front broken, the other companies will be moved to follow your example? Very well, negotiations will be ordered, to be carried out by a representative of the Council within the legal term of time. May I congratulate you, Gentlehomo Sa, upon your reasonable and sensible handling of a difficult situation."

Again Sa smiled. "Which is more than any of my conferees shall do," he remarked.

"Now we come to the next point," Cullan's manner changed abruptly. "Your liberty was threatened, your persons put into danger, through the misguided efforts of a service officer. Do you wish to register an official complaint?"

Sa's smile grew broader. He put down his cup.

"Councilor, it is my impression that this particular matter is none of my affair, not does it concern

167

matters on Fenris in any way. I beg your leave to withdraw. The overzealous officer I leave to your discretion." He stood up, put out one hand to Samms.

"Gentlehomo, since our business here is complete, shall we go?"

Samms evaded that touch. He leaned forward, to stare past Sa . . . at Hogan? Or Lennox? It was Cullan who broke the momentary silence.

"Gentlehomo, if you believe that you have a private understanding with this officer, its provisions are now cancelled. You do not control anything or anyone that he desires. Furthermore he is no longer in a position where he can hope to bargain. Correct me if I am wrong, Commander."

Lennox continued to look straight ahead, past Cullan, out at the advance of the dawn. As Sa had appeared a few moments earlier, now he in turn was a little shrunken, diminished. Samms got to his feet.

"What about you?" the Fenrian's voice was ragged as he asked that of Hogan.

The ex-trader rested one hand as if to wave farewell. "Samms," he replied with all his old lazy lightness of tone, "I am about to make you a gift, a large, enticing gift, which no growing boy could possibly resist—Fenris. You will make a good deal now for those who backed us, of that I am reasonably sure . . . for two reasons. First, because Gentlehomo Sa has admitted he sees the writing on the wall of outer space and is ready to lead a vanguard of pioneers into a bright new era . . ."

Sa bowed urbanely, with a gentle chuckle.

"And secondly, since Fenris is now your undisputed preserve, you will do all you can to make yourself vip there. Which entails a certain continuing regard for the rights of your future co-workers and liege men. You leave with my blessing and a free field. Don't bother to inform me in return that you hate my insides, and now all the more for this withdrawal on my part. We are both well aware of that.''

A flicker of light in Samms' eyes. He ignored Hogan, bowed to Cullan. With a dignity Joktar could not deny him, he then took Sa's arm and they left together, already linked more than physically by a future both could visualize, even if those visions did not exactly coincide.

As the door panel closed behind them, Hogan added more briskly:

''End of chapter, perhaps of book.''

''That one,'' amended Kronfeld.''

''Now,'' Cullan once more regarded the spreading blanket of color in the sky. He watched that display a long moment before he spun his chair around to face Lennox ''We know,'' he said quietly, but with an emphasis which bit, ''everything, including much that you do not, Commander. But by what right under all the stars of this galaxy, or the next, dare you move against the Ffallian?''

13

LENNOX lost his detachment. His face screwed into a mask of hate.

"If you know everything, then you also know why."

"Yes, I know why. Because twenty years ago a man who was bringing with him an offer of the greatest gift our species could have, appealed to you for help in the name of friendship, and you betrayed him to his death."

"Oh, no," Lennox shook his head, "you can't fasten what *you* claim to be a crime on me, Councilor. I did what I had to do, what my loyalty, not only to the service, but all our kind, demanded of me. Nor will I deny that I agreed with every word of the orders I obeyed when I turned Marson in. He wasn't even human any more! What I did, I did for the good of every human being, in or out of space.

That traitor," his mouth twisted, "was a monster. What he came to offer was vile. You should thank whatever gods you believe in, on your knees, that he did not carry out his mission."

"One way of looking at it," Kronfeld's judicial evenness of speech was the more impressive in contrast to the other's hot vehemence. "That fanaticism has had official approval for quite a while. Only there's another side to the same story. Marson had, in the pursuit of his scout duty, made contact with the Others who we have long known shared our galactic space. The period of Marson's contact began involuntarily on his part because he answered a strange distress signal and became involved in a rescue. He could not be as inhuman as his orders demanded he be therefore he discovered that this other species was entirely different from the official descriptions circulated by his superiors. He then joined them, lived among them, and only because he learned something which would benefit both races equally, did he volunteer to return to human-held territory, knowing that such an act might well mean his death. He hoped that some man of good will would listen and examine his proof.

"He came as an ambassador. But before he had a chance to reach those who might have understood, he was caught and killed, the whole affair covered up. This ended the matter—for all-time your service believed. Then, fifteen-or-so years ago, there came a second attempt at communication. Because the situation on the other side was growing critical, though our short Terran life span does not limit those Others. This time the volunteer ambassadors numbered two, with a third individual brought to prove their point.''

Lennox's fingers plucked at the empty blaster's holster on his belt.

"A scout named Ksanga, had followed Marson's earlier orbit, been attracted into the same pattern of co-operation. He came back as pilot of a ship which landed on the planet Kris, two passengers on board, a woman and her child. He dared to return even though he knew that he was outlawed as no other wolfhead since the beginning of time. Unfortunately he was recognized on Kris, picked up by your police. He contrived to die before he was forced to betray those he had brought with him. How they escaped we shall never know. But eventually they reached Terra.

"The woman, although fully armed against the dangers her people could anticipate, was not immune to terrestrial disease. She died in N'Yok, in JetTown where she had found a temporary hideout. The child remained.''

Joktar put down his empty cup. Now he was as fascinated as the commander by Kronfeld's story.

"By Terran standards that child appeared to be about six years old, he was closer to twelve. And he had been provided with a mental block for his own protection. In JetTown he found a place for himself, eventually fitted into the pattern of the streets. Neither he, nor those about him, knew how important he was.''

Kronfeld picked up a paper, but he recited rather than read. "What was the driving motive behind Marson's return, Ksanga's sacrifice, and the woman's? Oh, I've heard all the wild tales the services have fostered through the years since our first contact with the aliens—"

"Wild tales?" Lennox spat between his teeth. "Just because you don't believe the truth?"

"What is the truth? That the aliens are immortal? That fact could be difficult for us to accept. But it isn't true. Not only can they die by accident, but also, though their life span is immeasurably longer than ours, they are mortal in the ordinary fashion. That they are our superiors mentally and physically? Yes, that gives us a feeling of inferiority which many little men find impossible to face. But they have also one overwhelming disadvantage on their side of the scales."

Now Lennox actually did spit. The droplet of moisture beaded on the dark surface.

"They want us!" his face flushed darkly. "They have to have us to breed."

Kronfeld regarded him somberly. "Fifty years ago," he said in a remote tone, "a hysterical and perverted man put his own interpretation on a secret report. Perhaps he made an understandable human error, under the infleunce of his warped background, perhaps he had another reason for what he did. He slammed a door for his whole species. But it is an axiom that truth can not be hidden forever. Other men have been searching for those hidden files, for the true meaning of that report ever since. Three years ago the real story came to those who dared to believe. All the garbled nonsense which Morre fed his followers was sifted. Then the facts underneath and the monstrous crimes he fathered on the aliens were discovered to be something quite different. Yes, these galactic neighbors must have another species allied with them for breeding, but that act does not follow the unspeakable pattern Morre pictured out of the vileness of his own evil imagination.

"The aliens are humanoid, but not human. They have voyaged the star lanes for a length of time we cannot measure. They were comrades-in-arms and good friends to other races who preceded us into space, those who built the ruins we now find on dead worlds, for we are new to come into an old, old region. But long ago their species suffered a mutation which has almost doomed them to extinction. If they mate among themselves, the resulting children are female only. If they mate with a kindred humanoid race, the children are the Ffallian, and all male.

"In turn the Ffallian may mate fruitfully with either human or alien and produce children of both sexes. And the children of that second generation, as the Ffallian themselves, will have an increased life span, certain distinct physical and mental advantages over our kind. A long time has ensued since the aliens have found a race with whom they could have common offspring, and the Ffallian grow fewer every year. So they were overjoyed when they discovered that we were a species they could—"

"Use to produce their half-breed monsters!" Lennox exploded.

"Half-breeds, yes, monsters, no! Very far from monsters. Luckily all minds have not been corrupted by Morre's poison. A woman of the aliens chose to mate with Marson. Their son is true Ffallian. She brought him to Terra after her husband's death to prove that point, beg help for her people. Now, years too late, we may succeed in making her mission worth while. We do not have the gifts of the aliens, but our sons and daughters will. As human time is reckoned it may take many years, but the Ffallian will increase in number, linking us with the aliens in a pattern of sharing which will give us both something close to immortality.''

''You're mad!'' There was horrified conviction in Lennox's answer. ''Try urging people to mate with monsters and see how quickly you'll have a war on your hands!''

''I said it would have to come slowly. We've already made a start. I head a colonization project in which we are educating a picked group. And we have pulled the whole subject out of hiding. The right kind of publicity is as good as the wrong kind, and we shall use the right.''

''You can't do it! They've fed you a prettty story and you've swallowed it. The real story is anything but pretty. Morre knew, he saw the results. You talk of supermen, he saw the devils that really issue from such cross-breeding.''

''Devils? You have seen one of these 'devils' too. In what way is he a monster? Does he resemble the ogres Morre dreamed up to support his edited records?''

Lennox's head turned, his hot eyes fastened on Joktar. And then, when none of them expected such a move, he launched himself straight at the younger man, his hands reaching for the Terran's throat. Reflexes trained on the streets moved in Joktar's defense. But he was borne back across the ledge until his head cracked against the unbreakable substance of the window. In a matter of seconds the Terran knew that he was battling for his life against a man in a frenzy, a man who scratched, tore, snapped teeth in a hideous attempt to maim and kill. A little dazed by the madness of the other's fury, Joktar fought back.

Then Lennox's dusky color deepened, he snarled and whined, as his head was forced back by an arm clamped under his chin, levering him away from Joktar. He clawed at the air, fought against that merciless bar of flesh and bone closing off his breath. Joktar raised a hand to dripping scratches on his cheek and watched Hogan choke the commander into submission.

There was a scuffle as Cullan summoned patrolmen, had the half-conscious Lennox removed. But Joktar had turned his back on the room. He was trying to blot out what he had just heard. That old chill thrust of loneliness struck into him . . . spreading . . . walling him off from the men in the room behind him, and in a measure from the room itself.

Monster . . . half-breed! Lennox had fastened those tags on him. And there would be hundreds . . . millions of other all around the galaxy to raise the same cry. He had been well tutored on the streets. Since the beginning of the human species there had been in them that dark and evil urge to turn upon and rend the one who was different, to hunt him down with a mob. And to be the hunted awoke in Joktar a wave of sheer terror which washed through his brain.

Loki's sun was up now. A blaze above the golden

brown of he sea . . . warmer than the sun which touched snow drifts on Fenris. The life of the streets had existed at night, there were few times when he had really looked at the sun.

A golden planet, a world where the sun was warm and kind . . .

Joktar heard movements in the room, closed his ears to them. They were all men there and he was something else. In those few moments of speech Lennox had raised a barrier between him and every living being he had ever known.

Sun on the waves . . . a golden world . . . well, he would have to face those others, and his future some time. Joktar turned his back to the sun, his face to the room.

Only Hogan stood there. He was studying the younger man with the same searching measurement he had once used on Fenris. He spoke softly.

"But it isn't that way at all, you know. Don't let that poison Lennox spouted mean anything. You aren't alone."

"Half-breed," Joktar said the ugly word.

"Ffallian," Hogan corrected. "It is very different. I know . . . believe me, I know."

"How?" challenged Joktar.

"Do you think that your father and Ksanga were the only humans to join the aliens? Four years ago . . . I came back."

"But you were on Fenris . . . a trader!"

"Hiding out . . . just as much of a wolfhead as if I were Ffallian. I was waiting for Kronfeld to move. He had to find you. That you existed, we knew. *Where*—that we had to discover. Yes, Lennox was wrong, pitifully horribly wrong. Do you believe me?''

And Joktar, seeing what lay in the other's eyes, was moved to a conviction which banished all the wariness he had learned from his father's unpredictable breed.

MORE SCIENCE FICTION ADVENTURE!